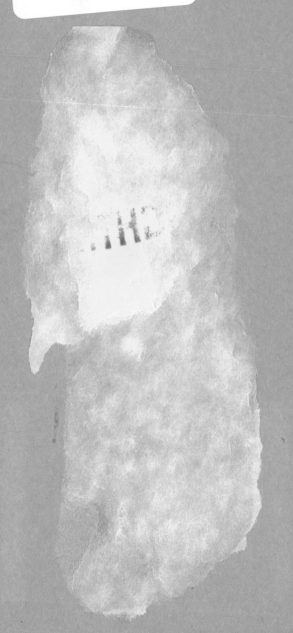

A Dream
With No Stump Roots
In It

A Dream
With No Stump Roots
In It
Stories by David Huddle

University of Missouri Press

1975

Library of Congress Catalog Card Number 74–22229
Printed in the United States of America

Library of Congress Cataloging in Publication Data

Huddle, David, 1942-
    A dream with no stump roots in it.

    (A Breakthrough book)
    CONTENTS: Luther.—The interrogation of the prisoner Bung by Mister Hawkins and Sergeant Tree.—Waiting for Carl. [etc.]
    I. Title.
PZ4.H883Dr [PS3558.U287]   813'.5'4   74–22229
ISBN 0–8262–0174–1

For Lindsey

Contents

Luther, 1

The Interrogation of the Prisoner Bung by
    Mister Hawkins and Sergeant Tree, 17

Waiting for Carl, 27

Rosie Baby, 35

The Proofreader, 59

A Dream with No Stump Roots in It, 107

Luther

They sent me to Africa to preach the word of God the Almighty to the Black People. Vera and me already had our hearts set on going to Ashtabula, Ohio, when the letter came, telling us we had been selected to go to Africa. Congratulations, it said.

Eleanora, our little girl, wasn't quite four years old then. Vera cried and cried about Eleanora. Vera said she didn't mind her and me going to Africa to do the work of the Lord, because we were old enough to look after ourselves. But she didn't know what was going to become of Eleanora over there in the jungle. Lord, Lord, she said and cried all night. And I wasn't no help to her.

The next day I went over to the old lady Gearhart's house and borrowed a big stack of her National Geographic Magazines to take home for Vera and me to look at. The old lady Gearhart was Vera's and my landlady for a year or so after we got married. I knocked on the door and told her I was going to Africa and could I please borrow some of her magazines? She stood there wheezing with her nervous allergy, trying to get the screendoor unhooked. Finally she did let me in and then stood there, breathing hard, in that old, dusty, half-dark hallway.

"Luther, what in the name of Heaven are you going to do in Africa?"

I told her that the church was sending Vera and me over there to do some missionary work to try to help the Black People. She shook her head and said that if the church wanted to help the Black People, it didn't have to go all the way over to Africa to do it. But it wasn't none of her business, she said, if I wanted to go to the North Pole to help the Eskimos. Lord knows she wasn't going to stand in my way. She said for me to help myself to the National Geographics. She started back toward the kitchen, but then she stuck her head back out into the hallway and hollered at me.

"What does Vera have to say about you and her and that baby going to Africa?"

"She don't like it much," I said.

"Well! I reckon she don't." I heard the kitchen door swing shut again, and I heard her wheeze to herself, "I'll just bet she don't like it very much."

Mrs. Gearhart's husband, the late old man Sam Gearhart, had started keeping all the National Geographic Magazines on the shelf in the bathroom. Old lady Gearhart used to warn me not to get to reading in there like her husband used to do when he was alive. She didn't want to have the other boarders waiting outside while I read an article in there. I tried to tell her that I wasn't in the habit of reading while I was in the bathroom, but I don't think she listened to me. Women like that don't listen to people too much anyway, and if they do, it usually means they're mad about something or fixing to get that way right shortly. Every once in a while when I'd stay in that bathroom a little longer than she thought was the necessary amount of time, I'd hear her come wheezing up the steps. She'd bang on the door and yell, "Luther, you're not reading in there, are you, son?"

I'd holler out, "No, Ma'am," but the truth was that I did read in there a little bit every now and then. I didn't think it hurt anything.

Vera didn't seem to take much interest in the National Geographic Magazines. When I found an article or a picture that I thought was of particular interest and I showed it to her, why she'd just look at it and then look away and say "Um hum," like it wasn't anything important to her. Once I showed her a picture of a big crowd of Black People standing around this grass hut kind of a thing. The children in the picture all had their stomachs poked out, and I was explaining to Vera that what caused it was not eating the right kind of food. Malnutrition. Something caught her eye, and she took the magazine right out of my hand, looked at it real close, and said, "Luther, some of these people in this picture are women!"

I looked at the picture again while she was holding it, and I could see what she was talking about, them savages with their bosoms sagging down like that, but I didn't want to make anything out of it. So I said, yes, I guessed some of them probably were women. Vera's hand started trembling, and she kept looking at me like I ought to be able to do something about it. As if I could go over there and make all of them savage Black women start wearing brassieres! Finally she stopped looking at me and dropped the magazine and picked up Eleanora and ran upstairs to the bedroom and slammed the door. I knew she'd be crying, but I didn't even try to go to her.

Brother Maxwell was the one whose place I was going to take. They brought him back to the United States so that he could help to train his replacement. Which was me. Brother Maxwell was a great big fat-cheeked, red-eyed, bald-headed Child of the Lord, with a voice so loud and so low that it sounded like it had rumbled up out of the bottom of the ocean.

Brother Maxwell started sweating in this room they put us in, even though it didn't seem hot to me. He took off his coat and his tie, and he rolled up his sleeves on his big, hairy, red-freckled arms. He asked me if I wouldn't like some chewing gum, and I told him I didn't care for any, thanks. He put three sticks of Juicy Fruit in his mouth, one at a time, and then he started talking.

"Now, Luther, your African Black Person is the very same product as your Mississippi Black Person, or your California Black Person, or your New York City Black Person. One Black Person is just like another one, and they are all mighty hard to do anything with, because they won't listen to you."

Brother Maxwell looked at me to see if I knew what he meant, and he must have thought I did because he shifted his wad of gum to the other side of his mouth and went on.

"Now one thing a Black Person needs is Jesus. Jesus can do more good for your average Black Person, in the way of being a steadying influence on him and keeping from running amuck, than anything you can give him. The Bible itself won't have much effect on your run-of-the-mill Black Person unless you show him what to do with it, make it meaningful to him, as the man says. What I mean is, you got to open it up and show him what's on the inside. Show him the red parts where it is the direct and literal speech of the Lord Jesus Christ, because if there's one thing a Black Person likes, it's pretty colors. You got to read some to him and preach to him a little bit so that he can get the feel of the thing. And you got to get him to singing some hymns because nothing in the world works so effectively on a Black Person as good music.

"Then, of course, you got to get your Black Person acquainted with the idea of Sin, and just exactly what it is to Sin, and what it will do to him when he does Sin, as he inevitably and obviously is going to do.

"But now the main thing is—and this is important; I'm telling you from my own experience in Africa and elsewhere—you've got to take these little white New Testaments like this." He showed me one that he plucked up out of his jacket pocket, and he poked it over toward me like it was perfectly obvious that I wanted to see it.

"These little white buggers here will flat get you some results out of your African Black Persons," Brother Maxwell said. "You can wave your regular black-cover Bible under his nose all day long, and he will just ignore it and you both. But you let him get a peek at this little white, imitation-leather, pocket-size, red-lettered New Testament, and he'll pay some attention to what you tell him."

I listened pretty close to what Brother Maxwell had to say, because I think it is important to get started out right, no matter what it is you are about to do. Brother Maxwell seemed to get more and more nervous and fidgety the whole time he was talking to me. Sweat kept pouring off of him. Once he spit out his wad of Juicy Fruit into an ashtray and put in three fresh sticks of chewing gum.

All of a sudden Brother Maxwell said, "Excuse me, Luther," got up, picked up his coat, and left the room. I waited a long time for him to come back, but he never did come. Finally I went on home and told Vera about Brother Maxwell and what all he'd said. She didn't have anything to say. She just looked at me with that new look she seemed to be developing for me whenever I brought up anything concerning us going to Africa. I took the baby outside in the back yard and played with her until it got dark and time for supper.

As a usual thing, when we've finished eating supper and put the baby to bed, I like to sit in the kitchen with Vera while she's cleaning up the dishes. Sometimes we talk to each other, if we have anything to talk about, but most of the time we just keep quiet and enjoy each other's company without saying much. On this particular night, we had absolute silence. I was picking my teeth and not thinking about anything in particular, like I usually do, when all of a sudden Vera turned around and looked at me and said, "Luther, we just can't take that baby to Africa!" She'd been standing there with her back to me, crying all that time, and I didn't even know it. I stood up and went over to her and gave her a hug and smoothed down her hair. I told her I'd talk to them over at the Bible College about it tomorrow.

It wasn't no use, of course. When I went in to see the Bishop and he gave me that smile of his, I knew it wouldn't be no use in talking to him. But I went ahead with it anyway because I had told Vera that's what I was going to do. I said my piece, and then, of course, he talked me out of it. I remember him saying that I was a "man of unshakable faith and perseverance," and that I was the best man to do it because of my "qualities." I stopped listening to the Bishop then and just waited for him to finish so I could go on home and tell Vera that it wasn't no use.

I thought we never would get to Lubumbashi. By the time we got to Nairobi, the baby had already cried all the tears she had stored up for the next ten years. And it is useless to describe the mood Vera was in. When we landed she had a line of perspiration drops on her upper lip, and around the arms of her new pink traveling dress were these big dark circles of sweat. It seemed to me like I had been having nightmares for about two months without a break.

I started looking for this Deacon Johnny T'Tenrab the minute I stuck my head out the door of the airplane, but I didn't see anybody I thought was him. We just went along the way it seemed like everybody wanted us to go until we got inside this waiting room where they had fans hung down from the ceiling, turning so slow and feeble, there wasn't even a breeze. Waste of electricity, as far as I was concerned.

While I was sitting there waiting for Vera and the baby to come back from the rest room, this very well-dressed Black Person came in the doors and looked around like he certainly expected to be welcomed by somebody a whole lot more important than anybody he saw in that waiting room. He had on this white linen suit with a white tie to match and a light-blue shirt. When he saw me, he walked straight over to me. I stood up and looked him square in the eyes and said my Swahili phrase Brother Maxwell had taught me.

He turned it over in his mind a second. I could see his lips tracing the words over, but he must have decided to ignore it because he said, "How do you do? I am the one called Johnny T'Tenrab. I assume that you are the Reverend Luther Woodruff?" I told him yes, that was me. We were shaking hands when Vera came over with Eleanora, who had finally quieted down and looked sleepy. The Deacon Johnny T'Tenrab took us to the Charles Hotel in a taxi. He sat up front with the driver, while Vera, Eleanora, and me sat in the back seat looking up at his rich black neck and the little circle of light-blue shirt collar above that fine white linen suit jacket on his shoulders. He pointed out various points of interest of the city of Lubumbashi to us along the way. He helped me carry the bags upstairs to our room, and then he left, saying for us to get some rest and he would meet us that evening at eight o'clock in the lobby of the hotel for dinner. When he closed the door, Vera didn't smile at me, but she did touch my hand to show me that things were maybe going a little bit better. We put the baby between us on the bed and went right straight to sleep without any trouble at all.

That night the Deacon Johnny T'Tenrab's teeth shone in the candlelight, and his tongue was pink and lazy when he talked and smiled. The Deacon ordered our food from the waitress in a low voice so that Vera and me couldn't hear what he said. We looked at each other because we knew that the reason he did it was because he was embarrassed. They've got their own kinds of food, and they don't like the same things we do.

The waitress brought these pretty little delicate glasses to us. Then she brought a dark colored bottle with a white cloth wrapped around it and set it down in a silver bucket full of ice. When she opened the bottle, there was a pop that made everybody in the restaurant jump. She poured it into our glasses, and it was red as dark blood. The Deacon Johnny T'Tenrab had sat watching this girl pouring it, keeping his hands folded in front of him like the steeple of a church. When the waitress finished pouring, he nodded at her and she went away. He lifted his glass to Vera and looked first at me, then at her, and said, "To the lovely lady. May she find the Dark Continent full of smiles and laughter. May she find the people of Africa full of kindness and love. May she stay here in our country long and live in happiness."

He lifted his glass and sipped with a face as solemn as if he had been standing at the altar blessing a collection plate. I took a drink out of my glass, and, of course, Vera took one out of hers, too, even though she was blushing red as a pickled beet. It tasted like something I had been waiting all my life to drink. My eyebrows must have shot up at the first taste, because the Deacon smiled at me and said, "It's quite good, don't you think?" I told him yes I certainly did think, and Vera giggled. Then we all three laughed the way you do when you're having a good time. The Deacon's teeth glistened in the candlelight, and his eyes danced while he told us about his acquaintance with Brother Maxwell, my predecessor.

"The Reverend Mr. Maxwell was a zealous man," said the Deacon with a smile playing around his lips. "His name is known here in Lubumbashi and all the way up the river to Kasonga. In almost every family where there is a young beautiful girl, you will find one of these." The Deacon took out of the inside of his coat one of the little white-covered, pocket-size New Testaments. "The Reverend Mr. Maxwell brought the word of God to many of us here," he said. And then he really did smile. I didn't see what was so funny about it, and I didn't like what I thought this Deacon Johnny T'Tenrab was getting at.

"Why is it just families with young beautiful girls?" I asked him. "Why couldn't it be just plain old families, with or without the young beautiful girls?"

The Deacon kept his smile and looked at me like a schoolteacher looks at a boy having trouble learning how to spell his own name. "The Reverend Mr. Maxwell was especially interested in recruiting young beautiful girls to be Nuns."

"Nuns!"

"Yes, the Reverend Mr. Maxwell decided that while Nuns were perhaps not necessary to the work of the church in the United States, they were vital to our work here in Africa. He set out to form one of the largest assemblies of Nuns in recorded history."

"I can't believe it," I said.

The Deacon Johnny T'Tenrab smiled his schoolteacher smile at me again. "You will get used to the idea after a while. If you will turn around slightly in your chair, you will be able to see the lady selected by the Reverend Mr. Maxwell to be the Mother Superior of our church's Nunnery." Candlelight flashed in the Deacon's eyes and on his black skin. I thought for a second that I was sitting at the table with the very Devil himself, but I turned around to look anyway, and Vera was already turned that way looking. "She is known to us as Mother Eboly," said the Deacon while Vera and me were staring at the woman.

Her bosom was what you couldn't keep from looking at, because her dress was bright yellow and red flowers, and it was cut lower than anything I ever saw. Her bosom stood up full and smooth like tight brown satin. Her hair puffed out around her head and made her look like the queen of all Africa. She smiled at us, and that made tingles run up and down my back. Then she took a piece of Juicy Fruit chewing gum out of her dress at the bosom. She unwrapped it while we were watching her, and she stuck out her tongue to take the chewing gum into her mouth so slow and so lazy that it seemed downright dirty to me. "Obscene," was what Vera said about it later in the hotel room.

When we turned back around to our own table, the Deacon was sipping the coffee the waitress had brought for all of us. He told us that tomorrow we would go to see the Nunnery.

The sun shines better in Africa than it does in other parts of the world, I think. Outside it was so bright and so clear that it seemed like I was seeing everything in God's good world for the first time. The heat didn't seem near as bad as it had yesterday, and I got right much pleasure out of just looking at everything out there around me. Even the baby was in a good mood. The Deacon Johnny T'Tenrab had on a light-blue pin-stripe suit, a pink shirt, and a little lavender scarf around his neck. As usual he was fresh as a silver dollar, and he seemed like he was feeling especially good this morning. We came to a street crossing, and the Deacon offered his arm to Vera. She blushed very red in the face and around her neck and ears, but she took his arm just the way a lady is supposed to do. She held on to it even after we had got across the street and were walking along the sidewalk again.

To get to the Nunnery we passed through these iron-barred gates that must have been twelve feet high. It was the only way into the place, which was surrounded by huge stone walls. Inside there was a garden, and you knew the minute you were inside because the smell of the flowers made it seem like you had just stepped into Heaven. Bright splotches of reds and yellows and blues and oranges and pinks were everywhere. There were all kinds of trees, too, most of them a darker green than the ones we have at home. The walkways were made out of millions of small round stones, and these pathways were light against the dark shades of green of the trees and grass and plants. The flowers dazzled us all, especially Vera, with colors and perfumes.

At the door of the Nunnery we were greeted by Mother

Eboly herself. The Deacon introduced us, and Vera cooled considerably from the good mood she had been in out there in the garden with the flowers and all. Mother Eboly wore a pure white robe that was open in a V at her neck down to the belt of her waist, and her voice was soft and low and sweet. It was very hard for me not to stare at that wide open space of brown satin skin; it seemed like it would ripple if you touched it. She led us through this long, tall-columned entrance hall, over what seemed like about four or five acres of marble floor, to the courtyard.

If I live to be a hundred and seventy-five I will never see anything like what we saw that day. There was a long pool of blue water, in the center of which was a fountain that shot up a white spray of water that came splashing down again into the pool. All around were more trees and flowers. But the main thing we saw was the Nuns. Tall, striking girls, every one of them was made as perfectly as if she had been a carved statue. And every one of them was naked as the day she was born! I thought I was going to fall over in a dead faint. Vera just looked straight ahead. The girls were playing in the water and giggling and laughing and splashing around like children. The baby, of course, didn't know the difference; so she went over and played with the girls around the pool. I noticed that several of the girls were lying down around the pool and studying the little white-covered New Testaments very seriously. The Deacon said, "These are the Nuns of the Reverend Mr. Maxwell."

We sat down on a stone bench and talked with Mother Eboly for a while. But I don't remember what we talked about. I just remember those Black Girls playing and giggling and splashing. And Vera sitting stone-faced beside the Deacon. I tried not to listen to anything except the fountain bubbling and Mother Eboly's voice.

Snakes drooled down out of the trees over the river. It was hot. The water reflected the heat up at us while the sun beat down on us like fire. Vera sat up front with the Deacon. The baby-sitter sat next to them, holding Eleanora in her lap. Next came the four thin, hard-muscled boat rowers. Then me. I sat in the back of the boat by myself.

Once where the river ran so slow you could hardly tell it was moving at all, and everything was quiet except for the oars stirring in the green-scum water, five crocodiles slapped down off the bank into the water. I jumped almost out of the boat, it startled me so bad. They were all big enough to swallow me whole, it looked like to me. The Deacon Johnny T'Tenrab had his shirt off and was pointing to one of the crocodiles swimming away from us like a fast-moving log. I remember seeing how the sunlight glistened silver on the Deacon's skin so that you could see the muscles moving underneath. What was the worst part of the trip up the river was the snakes in the trees, though. Once when I turned my head over to look at the other side of the river, I was staring one right in the eyes. I saw his black thread of a tongue flicker out at me, and I dreaded passing under every tree after that.

It was pitch-black night when we got to Kasonga. It seemed to me like we had come all the way up that river just to step out of the boat right into the middle of Hell itself. Everywhere there was fire making red shadows, people moving, children screeching like demons, and Black People laughing, jabbering, and shouting to each other. Eyes and teeth flashed fire all around us. The children all had to touch us with their little, black, pinching hands. All the young men in the village came to glare at us with the whites of their eyes making them look mad as black lunatics. I was the only one it seemed to bother, though. The baby-sitter took Eleanora by the hand and led her along, making all the village kids be nice to her. Vera walked beside the Deacon Johnny T'Tenrab with her hand on his arm the same way they did in the city. I was glad she didn't mind being there, and I was happy to see the proud kind of a smile on her face. It makes a man feel good to have his wife proud of him, and I guess it was right courageous of me to be bringing the Word of the Lord right into the middle of savage Africa like that. I reminded myself to think of that more often.

There was a storm in the night, too. I woke up when it sounded like a bolt of lightning was hunting for my body and had just about found it, lacking a foot or two. It couldn't have been raining any more if somebody had picked up the ocean and turned it upside down on that one little village. It was absolute, solid water outside. I looked out the door of the little hut called the "Rectory" they had put us in. The great huge trees that stood outside the village were being stirred and swirled and twisted and whipped up like all nature had gone berserk. God has run amuck, I said to myself. I admit I was scared to death, and didn't even think to kneel in prayer, which, of course, I should have done. But Vera and Eleanora were sleeping all curled up like they weren't about to be waked up, storm or no storm. I went and laid down beside them and cupped myself up against them. After a while I stopped shivering. I must have gone to sleep a little while later, because I don't remember anything after that.

I opened my eyes to sunshine and perfect, clean quiet, except for the voice of a child, high and clear, like the tinkling of a small delicate bell. Vera and Eleanora were not in the hut. I expected that they had already got up and gone to get their breakfast. I was hungry myself. I stood up and walked outside. It was cool, still early in the morning and the smell of rain was still lingering in the air. In the sunshine the village looked like an entirely different place from what it had seemed last night. All around the huts was the hard, flat ground, light-colored like sand on a beach. Surrounding the village was the forest in a thousand different shades of green, but speckled with light colors, red, orange, and pink, from flowers and blossoms. The leaves on the plants were still wet with rain, and sparkles like diamonds in the sunshine teased my eyes. In the shadow beside the Rectory hut, there was a little boy, humming to himself, playing with his pet lizard. There didn't seem to be anybody else around; except over at the other end of the village there was a tree with a bunch of kids squatting around it. When I got closer to it, I saw that there was a cage built around the tree, and then I saw the two big snakes, pythons I guessed they were, coiled and curled around the tree and each other so that you couldn't tell which one was which, but could just see a tangle of green and brown colored bulges of scales. Somebody had put a chicken in the cage with the snakes, and it was running all around the tree squawking. The two flat snakes' heads didn't move. But I got the impression that their eyes were following each and every move that chicken was making. These kids were just squatting around watching, like kids at home watch television. I asked them where everybody was. One little one who was squatted closest to me looked up at me like he was mad I had interrupted his attention from the snakes. He pointed at this path over on the edge of the village leading into the jungle. When I walked into it, the shadows of the forest swallowed me up the way I had always imagined a whale, if he was so inclined, would swallow up a man.

A little way into the jungle, I met Eleanora and the baby-sitter coming back toward the village. I was glad to see Eleanora, and I asked them where Vera was. They told me she was back up that way. I asked Eleanora to come with me to find her mother. The idea didn't appeal to her at all. She started whining and sniffling to go on to the village with the baby-sitter. So I said all right and let them go on. The way Eleanora was acting these days, you'd have thought I wasn't even her daddy.

A little farther up the path I started hearing these voices in a kind of chant. The path started going downhill, and then it went around a curve. And there they all were, the whole village of Kasonga, including Vera and the Deacon Johnny T'Tenrab. Everybody was standing around this mudhole kind of a thing, a big pit with very dark earth in it and little puddles of rain water from last night's storm. There was a smell, too—mud and rain, but something else in the air, something that I seemed to have been smelling all of my life but really had never quiet smelled before this one time. When I got there and stepped up into the circle around the pit, drums started clattering and chunking, just like they had been waiting for me to get there.

Over on the other side of the pit, beside Vera and Johnny T'Tenrab, this very tall, painted character stepped forward. I guessed he was the witch doctor of the village because of the way he was dressed. He had big round swirls of red and blue paint smeared all over his body and a sort of a helmet with ostrich feathers shimmering up out of it. He stood there in front of us, straight and at attention like he was one of the guards at the Tomb of the Unknown Soldier. All of a sudden the drums stopped. There was silence. The witch doctor spread his arms out, bowed, and looked across the pit at me.

"Good morning, Your Most Reverend Sir! I am the one they call the Clanger of Bells. I shall act as your host for our Saint Maxwell's Communion Service."

Bell Clanger stopped talking, and I guessed it was my turn to say something, on account of I was an honored guest and all. I stepped a little bit forward and started talking as loud as I could so they could all hear me.

"Good morning, Mr. Clanger of Bells; ladies and gentlemen. I am happy to be here to share with you and the citizens of this village the service this morning. My wife and I hope someday to have the privilege of your company at one of our services in America. I thank you with all my heart for welcoming us here among you."

I bowed then, and on the other side of the pit Bell Clanger bowed and spread his arms and stood up again straight. I jumped when the drums started up this next time. They were loud and driving in a funny kind of rhythm. Bell Clanger let out this chanting kind of a bellow, and everybody around the pit took it up and started slapping their thighs in rhythm with the drums. It must have been a specially designed chanting song to work everybody up into some kind of a hypnotic spell. There was a pulse to it like a heart pumping blood, faster and harder and winding up tighter. I saw Vera starting to move her hands on her thighs like everybody else, and, of course, the Deacon was moving like a man in a spell with his hands slapping his thighs and his head bobbing up and down with a wild, unchained smile on his face, his eyes closed. I just stood there because I wasn't sure what the exact proper thing to do was.

It was so quick, so unexpected, that I thought for a second that I had been struck deaf. The drums stopped in what seemed like mid air to me, and there was a silence that prickled my skin. Then in one swift, blinding, simultaneous gesture, they were all naked and standing still, waiting. There clothes lay on the ground at their feet. Almost every one of them held in front of him, clasped in both hands, a small, white, imitation-leather New Testament. They stood there with their bodies glistening black and silver in the sunshine.

Vera stood opposite me, beside Bell Clanger and the Deacon. I saw Johnny T'Tenrab's lips move, whispering to her, and I saw her eyes search across that pit for my eyes, find them, and then on her lips came the smile of the Devil that I recognized the instant I saw it. I wasn't even surprised when she deliberately unbuttoned her dress and stepped out of it, naked like them, but white as a piano key. She stood waiting, too.

The drums and the chant started again, stronger now, driving and pumping with the sound of blood and flesh billowing up through the rhythm. First, Bell Clanger stepped down into the edge of the pit. Then everybody started down, the Deacon and Vera, too, chanting and singing and smiling. Two slender Black Girls took me by the arms and urged me toward the pit. And I went down into it.

I shiver now to myself when I think about it down in there with mud smeared all over us, slick and wet and moist, a thousand bodies moiling and surging in that quivering mud of the earth. Fever burned my brain. I was a lunatic, and I did terrible things that I would never have done if I had stayed under the wing of the Lord like I should have done. I have been told that I rose up out of the mud and ran out of the forest and through the village, fleeing in a boat down the river by myself. I do not remember it.

I do remember somehow stumbling back to the garden at the Nunnery and into the cool marble palace to fall flat on my face before I could even get out to that courtyard again, to those girls and the pool and the bubbling fountain. I do remember hearing her soft voice and waking to Mother Eboly's smile and being caught up in the soft vision of her brown satin bosom. But the fever still burned in my brain, and I don't remember any more than that, not even when they came to get me. The church sent two of the brothers from the Bible College for me, old classmates of mine. Vera and the Deacon Johnny T'Tenrab brought them to me in the palace of the Nunnery. They say that I wept and wept when they carried me out.

It was when I took the National Geographic Magazines back to the old lady Gearhart that it struck me how far I had come from where I had been, before they ever decided to send me to Africa to preach the Word of the Lord God Almighty to the Black People. I was starting up the stairs in her house with my arms full of those magazines I had borrowed almost a year ago. The old lady Gearhart asked me how Vera liked it now that we were Catholics. I had to tell her that Vera didn't like it much. Which certainly was the truth if I ever told it. But then I tried to explain it to the old lady Gearhart how, when I was in the hospital, everybody seemed to forget about me and not come to see me, except just when they felt like they absolutely had to go and see old crazy Luther. But this Priest didn't forget me. He came to see me every day, and he talked to me like there wasn't really much wrong with me at all. I wasn't much better than a raving maniac, but this Priest came every day. One day I asked him if I could confess to him. He smiled at me and said, "Certainly you can, Luther!" I did confess to him, and I told him everything I had done, all of it. It was like I spewed up all the rotten, ragged pieces of my soul and bleached it white again.

I tried to explain all that to the old lady Gearhart, but you know how women aren't interested in really knowing the right reasons for things. She just wanted to know what Vera thought of us being Catholics. After I finished all my long story, she said, "I thought Vera wouldn't like it too much," and she went on back into the kitchen. I took the National Geographics back upstairs to the bathroom, and I left her a good, leather-bound missal up there, so that she might read for herself.

The Interrogation of the
Prisoner Bung by Mister
Hawkins and Sergeant Tree

The land in these provinces to the south of the capital city is so flat it would be possible to ride a bicycle from one end of this district to the other and to pedal only occasionally. The narrow highway passes over kilometers and kilometers of rice fields, laid out square and separated by slender green lines of grassy paddy-dikes and by irrigation ditches filled with bad water. The villages are far apart and small. Around them are clustered the little pockets of huts, the hamlets where the rice farmers live. The village that serves as the capital of this district is just large enough to have a proper marketplace. Close to the police compound, a detachment of Americans has set up its tents. These are lumps of new green canvas, and they sit on a concrete, French-built tennis court, long abandoned, not far from a large lily pond where women come in the morning to wash clothes and where policemen of the compound and their children come to swim and bathe in the late afternoon.

The door of a room to the rear of the District Police Headquarters is cracked for light and air. Outside noises— chickens quarreling, children playing, the mellow grunting of the pigs owned by the Police Chief—reach the ears of the three men inside the quiet room. The room is not a cell; it is more like a small bedroom.

The American is nervous and fully awake, but he forces himself to yawn and sips at his coffee. In front of him are his papers, the report forms, yellow notepaper, two pencils, and a ballpoint pen. Across the table from the American is Sergeant Tree, a young man who was noticed by the government of his country and taken from his studies to be sent to interpreters' school. Sergeant Tree has a pleasant and healthy face. He is accustomed to smiling, especially in the presence of Americans, who are, it happens, quite fond of him. Sergeant Tree knows that he has an admirable position working with Mister Hawkins; several of his unlucky classmates from interpreters' school serve nearer the shooting.

The prisoner, Bung, squats in the far corner of the room, his back at the intersection of the cool concrete walls. Bung is a large man for an Asian, but he is squatted down close to the floor. He was given a cigarette by the American when he was first brought into the room, but has finished smoking and holds the white filter inside his fist. Bung is not tied nor restrained, but he squats perfectly still, his bare feet laid out flat and large on the floor. His hair, cut by his wife, is cropped short and un-even; his skin is dark, leathery, and there is a bruise below one of his shoulder blades. He looks only at the floor, and he wonders what he will do with the tip of the cigarette when the interrogation begins. He suspects that he ought to eat it now so that it will not be discovered later.

From the large barracks room on the other side of the building comes laughter and loud talking, the policemen changing shifts. Sergeant Tree smiles at these sounds. Some of the younger policemen are his friends. Hawkins, the American, does not seem to have heard. He is trying to think about sex, and he cannot concentrate.

"Ask the prisoner what his name is."

"What is your name?"

The prisoner reports that his name is Bung. The lan-guage startles Hawkins. He does not understand this language, except the first ten numbers of counting, and the words for yes and no. With Sergeant Tree helping him with the spelling, Hawkins enters the name into the proper blank.

"Ask the prisoner where he lives."

"Where do you live?"

The prisoner wails a string of language. He begins to weep as he speaks, and he goes on like this, swelling up the small room with the sound of his voice until he sees a warning twitch of the interpreter's hand. He stops immediately, as though corked. One of the Police Chief's pigs is snuffling over the ground just outside the door, rooting for scraps of food.

"What did he say?"

"He says that he is classed as a poor farmer, that he lives in the hamlet near where the soldiers found him, and that he has not seen his wife and his children for four days now and they do not know where he is.

"He says that he is not one of the enemy, although he has seen the enemy many times this year in his hamlet and in the village near his hamlet. He says that he was forced to give rice to the enemy on two different occasions, once at night and another time during the day, and that he gave rice to the enemy only because they would have shot him if he had not.

"He says that he does not know the names of any of these men. He says that one of the men asked him to join them and to go with them but that he told this man he could not join them and go with them because he was poor and because his wife and his children would not be able to live without him to work for them to feed them. He says that the enemy men laughed at him when he said this but that they did not make him go with them when they left his house.

"He says that two days after the night the enemy came and took rice from him, the soldiers came to him in the field where he was working and made him walk with them for many kilometers and made him climb into the back of a large truck and put a cloth over his eyes, so that he did not see where the truck carried him and did not know where he was until he was put with some other people in a pen. He says that one of the soldiers hit him in the back with a weapon, because he was afraid at first to climb into the truck.

"He says that he does not have any money, but that he has ten kilos of rice hidden beneath the floor of the kitchen of his house. He says that he would make us the gift of this rice if we would let him go back to his wife and his children."

When he has finished his translation of the prisoner's speech, Sergeant Tree smiles at Mister Hawkins. Hawkins feels that he ought to write something down. He moves the pencil to a corner of the paper and writes down his service number, his Social Security number, the telephone number of his girl friend in Silver Springs, Maryland, and the amount of money he has saved in his allotment account.

"Ask the prisoner in what year he was born."

Hawkins has decided to end the interrogation of this prisoner as quickly as he can. If there is enough time left, he will find an excuse for Sergeant Tree and himself to drive the jeep into the village.

"In what year were you born?"

The prisoner tells the year of his birth.

"Ask the prisoner in what place was he born."

"In what place were you born?"

The prisoner tells the place of his birth.

"Ask the prisoner the name of his wife."

"What is the name of your wife?"

Bung tells the name of his wife.

"Ask the prisoner the names of his parents."

Bung tells the names.

"Ask the prisoner the names of his children."

"What are the names of your children?"

The American takes down these things on the form, painstakingly, with help in the spelling from the interpreter, who has become bored with this. Hawkins fills all the blank spaces on the front of the form. Later, he will add his summary of the interrogation in the space provided on the back.

"Ask the prisoner the name of his hamlet chief."

"What is the name of your hamlet chief?"

The prisoner tells this name, and Hawkins takes it down on the notepaper. Hawkins has been trained to ask these questions. If a prisoner gives one incorrect name, then all names given may be incorrect, all information secured unreliable.

Bung tells the name of his village chief, and the American takes it down. Hawkins tears off this sheet of note-paper and gives it to Sergeant Tree. He asks the interpreter to take this paper to the Police Chief to check if there are the correct names. Sergeant Tree does not like to deal with the Police Chief because the Police Chief treats him as if he were a farmer. But he leaves the room in the manner of someone engaged in important business. Bung continues to stare at the floor, afraid the American will kill him now that they are in this room together, alone.

Hawkins is again trying to think about sex. Again, he is finding it difficult to concentrate. He cannot choose between thinking about sex with his girl friend Suzanne or with a plump girl who works in a souvenir shop in the village. The soft grunting of the pig outside catches his ear, and he finds that he is thinking of having sex with the pig. He takes another sheet of notepaper and begins calculating the number of days he has left to remain in Asia. The number turns out to be one hundred and thirty-three. This distresses him because the last time he calculated the number it was one hundred and thirty-five. He decides to think about food. He thinks of an omelet. He would like to have an omelet. His eyelids begin to close as he considers all the things that he likes to eat: an omelet, chocolate pie, macaroni, cookies, cheeseburgers, black-cherry Jell-O. He has a sudden vivid image of Suzanne's stomach, the path of downy hair to her navel. He stretches the muscles in his legs and settles into concentration.

The clamor of chickens distracts him. Sergeant Tree has caused this noise by throwing a rock on his way back. The Police Chief refused to speak with him and required him to conduct his business with the secretary, whereas this secretary gloated over the indignity to Sergeant Tree and made many unnecessary delays and complications before letting the interpreter have a copy of the list of hamlet chiefs and village chiefs in the district.

Sergeant Tree enters the room, goes directly to the prisoner, with the toe of his boot kicks the prisoner on the shinbone. The boot hitting bone makes a wooden sound. Hawkins jerks up in his chair, but before he quite understands the situation, Sergeant Tree has shut the door to the small room and has kicked the prisoner's other shinbone. Bung responds with a grunt and holds his shins with his hands, drawing himself tighter into the corner.

"Wait!" The American stands up to restrain Sergeant Tree, but this is not necessary. Sergeant Tree has passed by the prisoner now and has gone to stand at his own side of the table. From underneath his uniform shirt he takes a rubber club, which he has borrowed from one of his policeman friends. He slaps the club on the table.

"He lies!" Sergeant Tree says this with as much evil as he can force into his voice.

"Hold on now. Let's check this out." Hawkins' sense of justice has been touched. He regards the prisoner as a clumsy, hulking sort, obviously not bright, but clearly honest.

"The Police Chief says that he lies!" Sergeant Tree announces. He shows Hawkins the paper listing the names of the hamlet chiefs and the village chiefs. With the door shut, the light in the small room is very dim, and it is difficult to locate the names on the list. Hawkins is disturbed by the darkness, is uncomfortable being so intimately together with two men. The breath of the interpreter has something sweetish to it. It occurs to Hawkins that now, since the prisoner has lied to them, there will probably not be enough time after the interrogation to take the jeep and drive into the village. This vexes him. He decides there must be something unhealthy in the diet of these people, something that causes this sweet-smelling breath.

Hawkins finds it almost impossible to read the columns of handwriting. He is confused. Sergeant Tree must show him the places on the list where the names of the prisoner's hamlet chief and village chief are written. They agree that the prisoner has given them incorrect names, though Hawkins is not certain of it. He wishes these things were less complicated, and he dreads what he knows must follow. He thinks regretfully of what could have happened if the prisoner had given the correct names: The interrogation would have ended quickly, the prisoner released; he and Sergeant Tree could have driven into the village in the jeep, wearing their sunglasses, with the cool wind whipping past them, dust billowing around the jeep, shoeshine boys shrieking, the girl in the souvenir shop going with him into the back room for a time.

Sergeant Tree goes to the prisoner, kneels on the floor beside him, and takes Bung's face between his hands. Tenderly, he draws the prisoner's head close to his own, and asks, almost absentmindedly, "Are you one of the enemy?"

"No."

All this strikes Hawkins as vaguely comic, someone saying, "I love you," in a high-school play.

Sergeant Tree spits in the face of the prisoner and then jams the prisoner's head back against the wall. Sergeant Tree stands up quickly, jerks the police club from the table, and starts beating the prisoner with random blows. Bung stays squatted down and covers his head with both arms. He makes a shrill noise.

Hawkins has seen this before, in other interrogations. He listens closely, trying to hear everything: little shrieks coming from Sergeant Tree's throat, the chunking sound the rubber club makes. The American recognizes a kind of rightness in this, like the final slapping together of the bellies of a man and a woman.

Sergeant Tree stops. He stands, legs apart, facing the prisoner, his back to Hawkins. Bung keeps his squatting position, his arms crossed over his head.

The door scratches and opens just wide enough to let in a skinny, rotten-toothed policeman friend of Sergeant Tree and a small boy. Hawkins has seen this boy and the policeman before. The two of them smile at the American and at Sergeant Tree, whom they admire for his education and for having achieved such an excellent position. Hawkins starts to send them back out but decides to let them stay. He does not like to be discourteous to Asians.

Sergeant Tree acknowledges the presence of his friend and the boy. He sets the club on the table and removes his uniform shirt and the white T-shirt beneath it. His chest is powerful, but hairless. He catches Bung by the ears and jerks upward until the prisoner stands. Sergeant Tree is much shorter than the prisoner, and this he finds an advantage.

Hawkins notices that the muscles in Sergeant Tree's buttocks are clenched tight, and he admires this, finds it attractive. He has in his mind Suzanne. They are sitting in the back seat of the Oldsmobile. She has removed her stockings and garter belt, and now she slides the panties down from her hips, down her legs, off one foot, keeping them dangling on one ankle, ready to be pulled up quickly in case someone comes to the car and catches them. Hawkins has perfect concentration. He sees her panties glow.

Sergeant Tree tears away the prisoner's shirt, first from one side of his chest and then the other. Bung's mouth sags open now, as though he were about to drool.

The boy clutches at the sleeve of the policeman to whisper in his ear. The policeman giggles. They hush when the American glances at them. Hawkins is furious because they have distracted him. He decides that there is no privacy to be had in the entire country.

"Sergeant Tree, send these people out of here, please."

Sergeant Tree gives no sign that he has heard what Hawkins has said. He is poising himself to begin. Letting out out a heaving grunt, Sergeant Tree chops with the police club, catching the prisoner directly in the center of the forehead. A flame begins in Bung's brain; he is conscious of a fire, blazing, blinding him. He feels the club touch him twice more, once at his ribs and once at his forearm.

"Are you the enemy?" Sergeant Tree screams.

The policeman and the boy squat beside each other near the door. They whisper to each other as they watch Sergeant Tree settle into the steady, methodical beating. Occasionally he pauses to ask the question again, but he gets no answer.

From a certain height, Hawkins can see that what is happening is profoundly sensible. He sees how deeply he loves these men in this room and how he respects them for the things they are doing. The knowledge rises in him, pushes to reveal itself. He stands up from his chair, virtually at attention.

A loud, hard smack swings the door wide open, and the room is filled with light. The Police Chief stands in the doorway, dressed in a crisp, white shirt, his rimless glasses sparkling. He is a fat man in the way that a good merchant might be fat—solid, confident, commanding. He stands with his hands on his hips, an authority in all matters. The policeman and the boy nod respectfully. The Police Chief walks to the table and picks up the list of hamlet chiefs and village chiefs. He examines this, and then he takes from his shirt pocket another paper, which is also a list of hamlet chiefs and village chiefs. He carries both lists to Sergeant Tree, who is kneeling in front of the prisoner. He shows Sergeant Tree the mistake he has made in getting a list that is out of date. He places the new list in Sergeant Tree's free hand, and then he takes the rubber club from Sergeant Tree's other hand and slaps it down across the top of Sergeant Tree's head. The Police Chief leaves the room, passing before the American, the policeman, the boy, not speaking or looking other than in the direction of the door.

It is late afternoon and the rain has come. Hawkins stands inside his tent, looking through the open flap. He likes to look out across the old tennis court at the big lily pond. He has been fond of water since he learned to water ski. If the rain stops before dark, he will go out to join the policemen and the children who swim and bathe in the lily pond.

Walking out on the highway, with one kilometer still to go before he comes to the village, is Sergeant Tree. He is alone, the highway behind him and in front of him as far as he can see and nothing else around him but rain and the fields of wet, green rice. His head hurts and his arms are weary from the load of rice he carries. When he returned the prisoner to his hamlet, the man's wife made such a fuss Sergeant Tree had to shout at her to make her shut up, and then, while he was inside the prisoner's hut conducting the final arrangements for the prisoner's release, the rain came, and his policeman friends in the jeep left him to manage alone.

The ten kilos of rice he carries are heavy for him, and he would put this load down and leave it, except that he plans to sell the rice and add the money to what he has been saving to buy a .45 caliber pistol like the one Mister Hawkins carries at his hip. Sergeant Tree tries to think about how well received he will be in California because he speaks the American language so well and how it is likely that he will marry a rich American girl with very large breasts.

The prisoner Bung is delighted with the rain. It brought his children inside the hut, and the sounds of their fighting with each other made him happy. His wife came to him and touched him. The rice is cooking, and in a half hour his cousin will come, bringing with him the leader and two other members of Bung's squad. They will not be happy that half of their rice was taken by the interpreter to pay the American, but it will not be a disaster for them. The squad leader will be proud of Bung for gathering the information that he has, for he has memorized the guard routines at the police headquarters and at the old French area where the Americans are staying. He has watched all the comings and goings at these places, and he has marked out in his mind the best avenues of approach, the best escape routes, and the best places to set up ambush. Also, he has discovered a way that they can lie in wait and kill the Police Chief. It will occur at the place where the Police Chief goes to urinate every morning at a certain time. Bung has much information inside his head, and he believes he will be praised by the members of his squad. It is even possible that he will receive a commendation from someone very high.

His wife brings the rifle that was hidden, and Bung sets to cleaning it, savoring the smell of the rice his wife places before him and of the American oil he uses on the weapon. He particularly enjoys taking the weapon apart and putting it together again. He is very fast at this.

Waiting for Carl

The insane winters in New York, particularly the days when the wind on Seventh Avenue became very nearly unbearable, brought Partridge his best business. So even though he was southern and therefore especially despised the cold, he nevertheless found it necessary to be outside stomping up and down the sidewalk, shivering and hunching his shoulders, to make appointments and to advertise. True, he rented a second-floor office across from the Taft Hotel, but he could afford to go there only when he had made appointments for the afternoon, because if he didn't advertise, he got no business and then had to sit alone playing solitaire. It was also true that he wore a good wool suit, a tasteful tie, and a Harris Tweed topcoat that gave him a spiffy appearance, but these had been bought and sent to him by his mother in Athens, North Carolina, along with a stern note about what to wear and what to eat during the cold weather. Even with Partridge's bald head and thirty-five years, his mother still considered him more or less a college boy, and it irked Partridge considerably that he could not be completely independent of her. His business simply did not prosper him. The hand-lettered signs he wore, front and back, were the only advertising he could afford. They read as follows:

KINDNESS
FOR
MONEY.
I WILL BE
GENTLE TO
YOU FOR

FIFTEEN
MINUTES
OR A HALF
HOUR.
REASONABLE
PRICE.

"How much?" a dumpy-looking girl asked him. She was cold and miserable. Her nose dripped so that Partridge wanted to reach over and wipe it for her. She looked like she had been on the street gritting her teeth against the wind for a long time.

"Not much." Partridge hitched up his signs and straightened his shoulders to try to cheer up the dumpy-looking girl. As usual he found himself feeling sorry for someone.

"How long have you been in New York?" he asked her. "Oh God!" she said and blew her breath into her hands to warm them. "Almost three weeks!" she said.

Then she burst into tears. Brisk citizens passing quickly along the sidewalk craned their necks to look at the miserable girl; one or two of them smiled. Partridge felt his heart give its customary lurch of compassion, and he observed himself ridiculously patting the girl on her lumpy shoulder.

"You'd better come upstairs right now," he said. "It won't be but a dollar. There's a special rate today."

He took her arm, or rather her elbow, and guided her into the building where his office was. He actually lifted some of her weight to help her as they went up the shabby stairway. Sometimes Partridge felt like he could just kill himself he was so mushy. "You mushy son of a bitch," he muttered to himself. So far that morning he had made only one other appointment for the afternoon, and he knew from the look about the man that he would not pay more than five dollars for Partridge's services. You just couldn't stay alive in New York on six dollars a day, though you could live for a week on it in North Carolina, he thought.

"What did you say?" the girl asked. Still she sniffled and gave a dreary appearance while they walked down the dim, musty-smelling hallway, but Partridge thought she had better control now. He took his hand away from her elbow and let her walk by herself.

"I said you talk like somebody from Michigan," he told her.

She brightened a little. "No, but that's pretty close. I'm from Toledo." She unraveled the scarf she had wrapped all around her head and neck and shoulders. Her hair, a dishwater blond color, sprung out from her head at various angles. It's a shame she's not pretty, thought Partridge while he fumbled with the rickety old lock of his office door. Still, she might have a good figure, he hoped, because he could see only the lumpy outside shape of her long, brown, sheepherder's coat. He decided that if the girl had even a halfway decent figure, he would compliment her on it to make her feel better.

"You don't have any heat in here," she informed him when they got inside his office; she wrapped her arms around herself and shivered visibly to show him what she meant. Also, she looked as though she might cry again. Partridge had to agree that his office did appear fairly bleak when you first walked into it, plaster crumbling from the ceiling and walls, nothing in it but a window, a used cardtable, and two mismatched, straight-back chairs.

"I'm from North Carolina myself," he said. He decided not to address himself to the problem of no heat unless she insisted on getting something out of him about it. Certainly it was true that he was from North Carolina, and occasionally he blamed his damnable mushiness on the facts that he was southern and that his mother was such a severe lady, a member of the DAR. Partridge had a deadly envy of people who had that good, abrasive Yankee toughness of a Massachusetts or a Brooklyn or a Connecticut upbringing.

"Do you mind telling me what's wrong?" he asked the girl. He smiled in a kindly way at her while he lifted his sandwich board up off his shoulders and over his head, then leaned them carefully against the wall. He pulled out one of the straight-back chairs for the girl and then sat himself down in the one closest to the window. The girl was fiddling inside her purse for the dollar. Finally she pulled it out, wadded up like an old gum wrapper. She dropped it on the cardtable in front of Partridge, sniffled, and sat down with a heavy clunking noise. She unbuttoned the top buttons of her thick coat, so that Partridge could see the blouse she wore, colored a bright, fire-engine red. Unfortunately, Partridge noted, the blouse contained a regrettable lack of bosom, and he knew that he could not compliment her on her figure without hurting her feelings. Partridge knew that if the girl had been pretty, it would have been easier for him to lift up her spirits. He knew a little bit about the despair that fogs up the hearts of people who are not attractive; he himself had a rather egglike face and a bad color about him, so that in his childhood members of his family had predicted that he would become a minister. He picked up the dollar from the cardtable, put it in his jacket pocket, and began shuffling the deck of cards he kept to entertain himself during the long hours when he had no business. A certain smell of the girl came across the table into Partridge's nostrils, and it wasn't good. She needs a bath, among other things, he thought.

"Well," the girl said, "in Toledo I was always respected by everybody as being a person who is deeply devoted to art." The girl looked him squarely in the eyes as she talked to him. "But since I have been in New York, I have had nothing but hideous things happen to me, from the time I got off the train until this morning when a man on Broadway spat at me and called me 'scum of the earth.'"

The girl pressed her lips together to keep from crying, and Partridge could tell that the man had hurt her feelings. He dealt out a hand of solitaire for himself while he considered the girl's plight. Anybody who does not look like a movie star and who is sensitive ought not to come to New York, he thought. Then he looked out the window beside him and watched the traffic spurting down Seventh Avenue. "I see," he said finally.

"But that isn't my main problem," the girl went on. "The worst thing is that I didn't have any money, and so I signed this contract to work in this film about the Pittsburg Ax Murders, and now I don't want to do it any more." She smiled at Partridge when she told him this, and he saw a certain vivaciousness in her expression that might have led someone to sign her up to do an ax murder or two.

"I see," Partridge said again. He thought that the girl seemed considerably happier now. He could have sworn he noticed a swelling of the bosom inside the fire-engine red blouse.

"Why don't you just go on back home to your mother in Toledo and ask for her help," he suggested pleasantly to her. Partridge had that weird southern sense of home and family, which he hated when he thought about it but which he had not got rid of in fourteen years of living in the city.

The girl laughed merrily, a good peasant kind of a laugh, deep and healthy in her chest. "Well, I could, I suppose, but I don't think I'd be happy that way." She leaned across the table toward Partridge so that he could smell her closer, and this time it was quite a good smell to him a musky, hair-spray kind of fragrance. "You see," she said, "I have already completed the first half of the film, and now I sort of have a taste for the thing. You know how sometimes you hate things, but at the same time you kind of like them?" She smiled at Partridge fully, and he had to admit that she appeared seductive to him now, her hair glistening a soft blond color that set off her green eyes in an attractive way.

"Yes, I know," he said. He had the ridiculous urge to reveal something of his secret, innermost self to her. So he blurted onward, "I'm like that about the kindness I sell. I don't really like to give it out the way I do, but I can't help myself. I just can't stop myself from doing it, if you know what I mean." He looked at her pleadingly. Then he added as an explanation for it, "I think it's because I'm southern and because of the way my mother is."

They looked at each other and smiled openly. It was a beautiful moment in Partridge's life, because even considering all the people to whom he had been kind—and there had been a great many—he could not remember one who had understood him so closely as he thought this wonderful girl from Toledo did now.

"Do you mind if I take off my coat?" the girl asked. "By the way," she said, "my name is Cynthia." She took a splendid-looking, long-handled ax from the inside of her coat and leaned it against the wall beside Partridge's sandwich board. Her figure, Partridge now saw as she stood up, was no less than magnificent, a tiny waist, good hips, beautiful balloon-like breasts, and slender legs like those of a seventh-grade girl. All of these qualities gave her the appearance of being a genuine star of the cinema.

When she sat back down across the cardtable from Partridge, he simply could not stop looking at her, except to make a play now and then in his game of solitaire. Across the cardtable an electricity generated back and forth between them that seemed to be warming the entire room. Cynthia put both her hands on the table, and Partridge had to restrain himself to keep from reaching across and taking them into his own hands. The two of them sat staring at each other for a long time, with Partridge occasionally playing a card and with both of them savoring the silence together. They were disturbed by some kind of a clamor outside his office, clattering noises of equipment being moved, preparations being made, men yelling at each other, and heavy things being dropped, but this stopped and the pleasant quiet came again. Partridge genuinely regretted it when the time came for his other appointment. He looked at his watch several times before he said anything to her, but finally he had to.

"I'm awfully sorry, Cynthia, but I have another client coming here now. He should be here any minute. Maybe, if you don't mind waiting until I've finished with him, we could . . ."

Cynthia smiled gently at him. "Is this client a short man with a bald head and a kind of convict look about him?"

"Yes," Partridge said, "that's him. Why? Do you know him?" A knock came at the office door, and he got up, reluctantly, to answer it.

"Yes, I think so," said Cynthia. She got up from her chair, too, rising with Partridge. She touched his arm as he passed her, going toward the door. "Thank you so much," she said to him. "You've been a great help to me." She brushed his cheek with her lips and the lurch Partridge's heart took was not one of feeling sorry for anybody on the face of the earth.

"You're very welcome," he said. Then he turned and opened the office door for his client. There in the hallway outside his door, he found an entire camera crew, complete with microphones and sound equipment, carbide lights set up on stands and ready to go, and a huge, triple-lensed sixteen-millimeter camera on a tripod facing him like a three-eyed Cyclops. His client, the short man with a bald head and a convict look about him, sat a little farther back in the hallway, slouched in a canvas folding chair and puffing impatiently at a cigar.

"Ready, Cynthia?" the short man barked.

"Ready, Carl," she said. Partridge watched her sweep the cardtable clean of his game of solitaire and then come toward him, ax in hand. He had to admit that she looked radiant.

"Lights," said Carl.

Rosie Baby

I was going to need a stick. The First Sergeant told me I had to keep all of those people from the village from getting in there. I said, OK, I guess I can get a shotgun from Sergeant Martin over at the supply tent. But the First Sergeant said, "No, you can't shoot at them, the only thing you can take out there is a pistol, .45, with a cord fastened to the handle and looped around your neck because I don't want you losing that weapon out there and then maybe getting shot with it."

"But I still can't shoot at them?"

"No, Kramer, you can't. Not unless you get backed up into a corner where you can't get out any other way."

"How am I supposed to keep them out of that garbage dump if I can't shoot at them?"

"You just stand there and convince them that you're too big a man for them to fool with."

"Yeah, Sarge, but I mean really how am I?"

"Kramer, I don't care how you do it. The old man said that you have to keep them out of there and that you can't shoot at them. He didn't say how you was to do that. So I guess you better figure out a way of doing it."

Well, I needed a stick. That garbage dump was one square mile of mud and stagnant water and rotten piles of U.S. Army trash. It was on the edge of our base camp, but it was also on the edge of one of their villages. Driving out there in the jeep, we passed through the village, and they all looked at us; the kids waved and yelled at us to get us to throw C-rations out for them, and the girls didn't look at us at all, and the old people frowned, except when they were selling something—then they smiled, even the girls and the old people smiled. And right in the middle of the village, over the smell of their marketplace and their cooking and their garbage, we could always smell our own garbage dump. I'd seen it before, and there was always a big bunch of people from the village out there. All of them went down into that stinking mess, moiling around through the piles of trash to drag out anything they could carry. That stuff was like gold dust to them; they could use almost anything we threw away. The kids got the best stuff out of there, but the old people were good, too, and even some of the girls went down in there. One of the kids who doubled as a shoeshine boy was known to be the best of all of them at getting good stuff out of that garbage dump; I used to call him Fireball, and I used to get him to shine my boots when I went out there before. But I couldn't keep those people out of there without something besides a .45 pistol that I wasn't ever supposed to use anyway.

I had already met Rosie, too, because everybody who went out there knew her, or at least had seen her sitting cross legged, buck teethed and still pretty, on her old rusty ice chest by the road. Usually beside her sat the little baby girl, Rosie's friend, that we all called Knothead. Rosie sold beer and Coca-cola to the truck drivers who came out there to dump the loads of garbage from the base camp. They took their bottles on their way into the dump and gave her the empties on their way out. Rosie usually had four or five girls who worked for her as assistants, delivering the bottles to the truck drivers and then talking to them to keep them happy. But it was Rosie who ran the operation. She opened the bottles, popping the tops off and laughing at the sound it made, and then taking the money and making the change from the wad of bills she kept in her pocket. Rosie wore a light cotton pajama outfit, of no particular color, that showed her belly to be a little too fat, and the drivers teased her about it sometimes. They would pull the big deuce-and-a-half trucks up beside where she sat and hang their sweat-dirty arms down out of the truck windows to talk with her until the next truck came up behind to wait his turn and, finally, tired of waiting, come down hard on the horn:

"Hey, man, what you blowing at?"

"You better get on up that road, Jack. They got work for you to do back there."

"Man, you don't know what work is. What you trying to tell me?"

"Get on, Jack! I ain't going to wait on you all day."

"Bye, Rosie, baby! See you tomorrow."

It didn't take me long to figure out what was going on out there, and the first couple of days went pretty good. I had my stick that I had made out of about three feet of a broom handle that I cut off and drilled a hole into the end of and put a leather strap in so I could loop it around my wrist, because you don't ever want to lose your weapon in a situation like that. But I didn't ever have to use it. After I ran them all out of the dump in the morning when I first got there, nobody tried to get back in. I took off my shirt and walked around in the sunshine a while. And then it got hot so that I found a place in the shade not far from where Rosie sat. I stayed standing up there that whole first day, but then I saw that there wasn't any need to do that. So I sat down on a piece of an old busted oxcart that Rosie sent some of the kids to get for me. I got three or four free boot shines those first days because all the shoe-shine boys took a liking to me. The old people thought right much of me, too; they squatted around in groups and grinned over at me every once in a while. Most of them didn't have any teeth, or if they did have teeth, they were all black and rotten from chewing that stuff that they all chewed. All of us, the kids, the girls, the old people, and me and Rosie sat waiting for it to be time for me to go back in to the base camp for the night. Then I would be gone, and they could all go in to the garbage dump and get whatever it was that they wanted out of there. Every now and then I'd see them point to where a truck was unloading and hear them get to jabbering among themselves about what kind of a mighty fine thing it was that had just got thrown out of that truck. It was hot out there, and it stunk pretty bad. But I didn't have to move around very much. And I got used to the smell after the first couple of hours.

"Pretty easy job, huh, Rosie?"

"Sure, GI. Beaucoup easy."

"Yeah."

"You want beer, GI Kramer?"

"I got no money, Rosie."

"OK, no money, GI. You want beer, Coke—I give to you. OK?"

"Yeah, sure! Thanks, Rosie."

"No sweat, GI Kramer. You friend of me, friend of Rosie."

The First Sergeant said for me to come see him every day when I got back from out there. I went into the Orderly Room and stood around for a while until he noticed I was there. He said how are you doing out there, Kramer? I said just fine, Sarge, and he said good, good. Then I started out the door, and he said, "Uh, Kramer—"

"Yeah, Sarge?"

"You remember what the old man said, don't you, Kramer? Don't shoot at them. You got to keep them out of there, but don't shoot at them."

"Yeah, I remember, Sarge. It's no problem. They like me out there. They do what I tell them to do."

"Good, Kramer, good. It's important to remember, though. They is an awful lot of spooks running around here just waiting for somebody to do something wrong. You never know what rank they are—might be anything from a PFC to a colonel—but they sure can put some trouble on you, if you do wrong and they find out about it."

"Yeah, Sarge, I know it's important. I remember every day."

"OK, Kramer. I'll see you tomorrow."

The First Sergeant was a pain—not too smart and getting old and all. They said he'd been in Korea and World War II, both. But I liked him OK. He gave me extra duty only once or twice, and he gave it to everybody else in the company a whole lot more than me. So I liked him OK.

"Rosie, I told my First Sergeant what a nice girl you are. He says he wants to see you. He says he's gonna come out here and play with you tomorrow."

"Huh!"

"You'll like him, Rosie. He's got hair all over his old nasty self except for on the top of his head. He's an old man, beaucoup years. Good man for you, Rosie."

"I think maybe he better man than you, Kramer, baby. You tell First Sergeant come out play with Rosie. I give him good time. I give you nothing, Kramer, baby."

"Now, Rosie, you be nice to me, or I'll show you just what a good man I am."

She didn't say anything to that. Just stared at me with that half-smile of hers that was two-thirds of her conversation anyway. I did notice her right hand twitch just a little, but I thought she'd done that because of the flies that bothered us all the time out there.

"Rosie, where's my stick?"

She kept looking and not saying anything. I looked around me slow and even so as not to seem like anything special had happened. A bunch of shoeshine boys was squatted in conference behind me, but they weren't paying any attention to me, and neither were the old people or Rosie's girls, not even the little girl, Knothead. They would have thought I was a fool to ask where was my stick.

"Rosie, did you—?"

But she was talking with one of the truckdrivers. I didn't want to make it look like I needed that stick so bad. So I just pretended that everything was the same as before. Except I did walk around a little bit to see if I couldn't find it somewhere. Nobody seemed to notice that I didn't have it. Then I heard Rosie holler out, "Hey Kramer, baby, you want beer?"

"I got no money, Rosie." I always said that whenever she asked me if I wanted something to drink. I was looking with my back to her out over the dump where the only person out there then was a truckdriver.

"No sweat money."

"Yeah, thanks, Rosie." I heard her pop the top off the bottle.

The little girl, Rosie's buddy Knothead, came over to

where I was and put the cold bottle of beer in my right hand. I wasn't paying much attention to her on account of watching that lonesome truckdriver out there in the dump. Then she put the stick—my stick!—in my left hand. I looked down at Knothead, but she was already turned and baby-waddling back toward Rosie. Rosie was looking over at me still with that half-smile of hers. It seemed like she meant it to be more than just a joke, but I didn't know what it was all about. Or maybe I did know, because, now that I thought about it, I'd seen women look that way before.

"Yeah, thanks, Rosie." I felt better now. Things were going smooth now, like the skin on Knothead's bare little rear end. I smiled back at Rosie and took off my shirt to get a little of that warm sunshine.

That spook, Gartley, had the thickest glasses of anybody I ever saw in my life. He was young, maybe twenty-five or thirty, and he didn't act like much of a soldier. But the First Sergeant acted like he was a field-grade officer. I'd come in the Orderly Room like I did every evening, and the First Sergeant had been waiting for me like he never had done before. He asked me if I had done any shooting out there at the garbage dump, and I told him no, I certainly had not. He said that there was a spook outside waiting to see me, and I said, "Oh." The First Sergeant waited a minute to see if I would tell him anything else that might give him a clue as to why that spook wanted to see me, but I didn't say anything. So he took me out and introduced me to the spook.

"Sir, this is Corporal Kramer. Kramer, this is Mr. Gartley. Mr. Gartley is with the Army Intelligence people."

"Yes, yes. Of course. Hello, Kramer. Thank you, First Sergeant. That's all. Thank you. I want to talk with Kramer alone."

"You're welcome, sir." The First Sergeant left us standing out beside the Orderly Room where he'd taken me to meet the man. The man, Mr. Gartley, showed me an identification card in a little plastic imitation leather case. He didn't say anything, and he kept holding it up there in front of my face for me to look at, so that I finally said, "Uh-huh."

He snapped the little case shut and put it in his pocket. Then he took out a little green notebook and looked in it like he didn't want me to see what was on the inside but like he wanted me to know that there was something in there that I'd like to see, too.

"Corporal Kramer?"

"Uh-huh—I mean, yes sir?"

"Corporal James T. Kramer, R-A-1-5-8-6-4-9-2-1?"

"Yes sir?"

"Kramer, you understand that you have an important job? He put the notebook back into his pocket. I wondered what else he had written about me in there besides my name and service number."

"What's that, sir?"

"Guarding that garbage dump, Kramer. That is your job, isn't it?"

"Yes sir, that's my job."

"Good. Very good, Kramer. I wanted you to know that it is an important job, and that a significant number of lives depend upon your performing your duties to the very best of your ability. Those people must be kept out of that garbage dump."

"Yes sir."

"But, of course, you understand that there's to be no firing of weapons out there, except in cases of extreme emergency. We do not wish to alienate the people of that village. You've had all that explained to you, I'm sure. You seem to be an intelligent man, Kramer. I'm glad you were chosen for this job. I have every confidence in you and your ability to handle the job."

"Yes sir. They like me pretty well out there."

"Excellent. I think we shall get along very well, Kramer. I'll be coming out in a few days to take a look at how you handle this job. And I expect we shall develop a highly satisfactory working relationship, don't you, Kramer?"

"Yes sir."

"Good, Kramer. Very good. Thank you. You may go back to your duties now."

I saluted him even though I didn't know for sure if I was supposed to or not. He saluted back, but he knocked his glasses crooked when he did it. So I turned around and walked off real quick to keep from embarrassing him. But I stopped before I got back to the Orderly Room steps, and I watched him climb into his jeep. He had a short, stubby little dude of a driver that didn't even look at him, just kept on reading his funny book and smoking his cigar. Gartley didn't look at the driver, either; he just climbed in the shotgun seat, looked straight ahead, and told that driver where he wanted to go. The driver didn't say anything, just shifted his cigar in his mouth, folded up the comic book and put it in his hip pocket, started the jeep, and took off. That driver must have worked out with weights some time or other; his hands and arms were so big and hairy, the steering wheel of the jeep looked like a toy clutched in his fists.

"What did that spook want, Kramer?"

"I can't tell you, Sarge. Classified."

"Oh. I see."

"But I'll tell you this much, Sarge: That garbage dump is a whole lot more important than you or me thought it was."

"It is? You know, I thought it might have been when I first heard about it. Tell you what, Kramer. I'm going to take your name off the extra-duty roster while you got this job. And if I was you, I wouldn't do nothing wrong, at least not for a month or so. Them spooks threw a good buddy of mine, old Master Sergeant Jones, completely out of the army on account of they caught him in a dempster-dumpster with a WAC. That must have been back in 1961 because I know we was stationed together at Fort Polk, Louisiana, at the time. They said he was a security risk."

"Yeah, Sarge."

"Kramer, baby, I see you bring stick today. I worry. I think maybe you lose stick like yesterday."

"Yeah, Rosie, I know you worry about me. I worry about you, too. I worry all the time about you, girl." It was getting hot quick this morning so I took off my shirt a little earlier than usual. Rosie cocked her head at me like a chimpanzee.

"What you worry about me, Kramer, baby?"

"Oh, I worry about maybe you're lonely, don't have anybody to talk with at night."

Rosie laughed at that, laughed with her head thrown back. And Knothead and the girls and the shoeshine boys saw her do that, and they started laughing, too, and jabbering among themselves. Me and the old people kept quiet. But I couldn't stand that for very long.

"Rosie, what is it that you think is so funny that makes you have to laugh like a fool?"

She came over to me, smiling, or half-smiling now, and ran her finger light over my chest until goose bumps came out on it even in that hot sunlight.

"Kramer, baby, I say you have very white skin like baby-san. Very funny, huh?"

"Oh. Yeah. Very funny." I walked off still seeing her eyes tracing along with her fingers, dark against my chest.

"Corporal Kramer, good morning."

"Morning, sir, how are you Mr. Gartley?" He was climbing out of his seat. His driver was already settling down with his leg cocked up against the steering wheel and a new funny book and a fresh cigar. I watched him roll the cigar over his tongue and light it.

"Excellent, thank you, Kramer. What are all these people doing standing around out here? It seems a bit extraordinary to see half of the village population out here at the garbage dump."

"Yes sir. Well, they don't do anything wrong. I keep them from going into the dump. So they just stay around here with me and watch the trucks unload. Then when I go back to the base camp in the evenings, they go in the dump and get whatever they want out of it."

"Yes. I see. Of course. Well, I guess they create no immediate danger. And they keep you company in the absence of American companions, don't they?"

"Yes sir, they sure do. If you'd like your boots shined, I recommend that little one over there, the one with the scar on his stomach. I call him Fireball because it takes him about an hour to do just one boot. He does a pretty good job, though. That little baby girl over there is Knothead. And that's Rosie. Rosie, how about a Coke for Mr. Gartley here. Mr. Gartley, this is Rosie."

"How do you do, Rosie?"

Rosie smiled and blushed at him, popped the top off the bottle, and handed him the Coke. Then she picked up Knothead, who was trying to untie Gartley's bootlace, and carried her back over to the ice chest to sit down. Gartley followed her. I put my shirt back on and walked over to have a talk with that jeep driver. I saw his nametag read *Jones*, and his one stripe on his sleeve said he was a PFC.

"How are you doing, Jones?"

I thought I'd ease up to finding out what I wanted to know. But I could tell he didn't like me interrupting his funny book. He looked me up and down good before he spoke back, and I could tell he wasn't too impressed by the fact that I outranked him by one stripe. He did finally take the cigar out of his mouth and answer me.

"About to work myself to death, Corporal. How about yourself?"

"I'm doing all right," I said. "Yeah, Jones, I know it must be rough driving an important man like this Mr. Gartley around." I waited a minute, hoping I'd get something out of him with that. But he didn't say anything, and he didn't grin or frown or anything. Just sat there and waited for me to get done with whatever it was I had on my mind that was keeping him from reading his funny book. Well, I wasn't getting anywhere by beating around the bush, so I decided to change my strategy.

"Jones, what do you reckon it is that Gartley wants out here?" I asked him straight out. He shifted his eyes over to look behind me. I looked back and saw what he was looking at. It was Rosie. She had her arm up fixing her hair, and her shirt was pulled up showing a little patch of her skin on her side. Then he looked back up at me and said with as straight a face as I ever saw:

"I don't know what he wants, Corporal. I don't ask no questions. That way, see, I don't have to fool around with no answers. It's a good system. Look at me for example:

I have worked my way up from the ranks to where I am now—a PFC—just by using that sysem. You ought to try it, Corporal, and see if it don't help advance your military career like it did mine."

He kept looking at me for a second after he finished saying that like he dared me to say something back to him. Then he started to try to find his place in the funny book again. But this shoeshine boy, one of Fireball's buddies, had been worrying him about would he like his boots polished the whole time we'd been talking. It finally got on Jones' nerves. He caught that boy's skinny little arms up in his big fists and lifted the boy up like he was a rag doll. The kid was surprised at first, but then he must have figured that Jones was playing with him like I did a lot with all those kids out there. The boy grinned at Jones and asked him for about the two-hundredth time, "Shoe-shine?" That got Jones really mad. He pulled the boy close to him and held that cigar, clamped between his teeth, right up against the kid's chest. The kid hollered at first just from the shock, and then he hollered for real when it had burnt him good. Jones let him fall then, and the kid laid there on the ground crying. I didn't want to see any more of that. I started to say something to Jones because it made me mad. But I figured anything I would have said would have made him that much meaner. I started walking around the edge of the dump to forget about it. It would look more like I was doing my job right if I kept moving.

When I got back from my walk, Gartley was sitting on the ice chest with Knothead on his lap and Fireball polishing his boots. Rosie had pulled my old seat, the piece of a busted oxcart, over beside him, and she was sitting talking to him with his thick-lensed glasses, too big for her, stuck down on the end of her nose. He was trying to write in his little green notebook, but it must have been hard for him without his glasses because he had it right up against his face so he could see what it was he was writing.

"How about a Coke, Rosie?" It was really getting hot out there, and I wasn't used to walking around so much.

"Sure, Kramer, baby, OK." She popped the top off the bottle and handed it to me.

"Thanks."

"Thanks, twenty *piastre*, Kramer, baby."

"Huh, Rosie? What did you say?"

"I say you pay twenty *piastre*, Kramer, baby."

"Oh."

"Thank you, Kramer, baby."

"Yeah."

Gartley put Knothead off his lap, reached over, and took his glasses off Rosie's nose while she was putting the money I gave her in her pocket. He put his glasses on and focused in on me.

"Well, Kramer, the time has come for me to go back to the base camp. I can see that you're doing an excellent job out here with these people; I'll include mention of your fine performance in my report. I think there was no need of emphasizing that you were not to shoot at these people; obviously you have no trouble whatsoever keeping them from entering the garbage area."

"Yes sir, they like me pretty well out here."

"Yes, well, keep up the good work." He climbed in the jeep beside Jones who was folding up his funny book and not bothering to look at either me or Gartley. "I shall be back tomorrow to check a little further into the situation. I shall expect to see you then."

"Yes sir. Thank you." But I didn't salute him. And I didn't speak to Rosie all the rest of that day, not until the next morning.

"Rosie, why did you charge me for that Coke yesterday?"

"What Coke, Kramer, baby?" She stopped chunking the ice into the old, beat-up ice chest to look at me.

"The Coke I got from you yesterday while Mr. Gartley was out here."

"What? Who Mr. Gartley yesterday?"

"Four Eyes Mr. Gartley!" I showed her with my hands in front of my eyes.

"Oh, him. Yes, he drink Coke."

"No, Rosie, I drank the Coke, and I paid you twenty *piastre*. Remember?"

"I don't understand what you talk about, Kramer, baby."

"OK, Rosie, OK." It was getting hot, and I was mad. I started to unbutton my shirt, but she came over to me and undid the last couple of buttons with her right hand. I watched her watch her hand on the buttons, going down to the last one. Then her hand caught, caught hold of the waist of my pants at the belt buckle and stopped there, her fingers cool against my skin, and I watched her watch—but then she jerked slack in the waist of the pants, and I saw her left hand flash and drop the chunk of ice against my belly and down too far—cold!—and she running—

"What the—??!!"

I had to reach down there and get that chunk of ice out while they all laughed at me, and Rosie and Knothead and Fireball danced around and even the old people and a truckdriver—

"What wrong, Kramer, baby? What you do? I don't understand."

"Rosie, if I catch you—"

"Kramer, what's going on out here this morning?"

"Oh, good morning, sir, Mr. Gartley." He was standing right behind me. I hadn't heard the jeep drive up, but there it was with Jones already slouched in the driver's seat reading. "Good to see you, sir. Rosie and I were just having some fun this morning."

"Yes, of course. I see you were. Well, listen now, Kramer. I made my report to the General last night. He's very happy with the job you're doing out here. Very pleased. By the way, when are you coming up for promotion?"

"In December, I think, sir."

"Yes. Well. Good. I think we may be able to do something for you before then, if you keep up the good work. I'll talk with the General and see what I can do for you."

"Thank you, sir."

"Yes. All right. Now here's what we've decided in our discussion of my report, Kramer. There's entirely too much paper—written or printed material—coming out of that base camp in these truckloads of trash. That material gets into enemy hands, and it provides them with intelligence information about our base camp and our operations. They can use that information against us. And we have to stop that, Kramer. Now starting this morning I want you to stop every truck that goes by here before it gets into that dumping area. And I want every scrap of paper taken out of the garbage before it is dumped. Do you understand, Kramer?"

"All the paper and all the trucks, sir?"

"Yes. All the paper and all the trucks, Kramer."

"Yes sir."

The truckdrivers weren't too happy about stopping and getting out and climbing up into the backs of those trucks to help me sift through that garbage. It took a long time to go through each one, and it wasn't long before they were backed up, one behind the other, in a line ten or twelve trucks long, waiting, and there wasn't any shade on that road. I tied my stick to my belt so as to be able to use both hands to go through the garbage with, but it kept banging up against my knees and getting in my way. About the middle of the afternoon, the part of the day that was the hottest, Gartley must have got tired from sitting in the shade talking with Rosie.

"It's time for me to go back now, Kramer. I'll be coming back tomorrow to give you a little more help with this thing. You're doing a fine job. Excellent. The General will be pleased. Bye, bye now." He climbed in, and Jones started the jeep.

I didn't say anything. I just waited until the jeep was out of sight, and then I climbed down off that truck I was on, and I went over to sit on my old seat, the piece of a busted oxcart, that Gartley had sat on all that day.

"Rosie, quick, girl, let me have a cold beer before I die right out here in broad daylight in a foreign land!"

"You dirty, Kramer, baby, beaucoup stink!"

"You sure are right about that. I wish somebody'd tell me how in the world I'm going to get that paper out of all the rest of those trucks. There must be fifteen of them waiting in that line. I can't even see the end of it."

She popped the top off of the bottle and looked over at me. "Maybe Rosie help you, Kramer, baby. You want Rosie help?" She brought the bottle over and put it cool in my hand.

"Rosie, I want help from anywhere I can get it. Yes,

Lord I want Rosie's help." I untied the stick from my belt and laid it down beside us. She reached down and picked it up. She jabbered at Fireball and three other boys, motioning them to stand up in front of me where I sat.

"Baby-san go look in trucks, get paper. OK, Kramer, baby?" I looked at those four shoeshine boys grinning at me.

"Yeah! Rosie, you are a genius. Why didn't I think of using those kids?"

Rosie jabbered at them, and the four boys ran off toward the first truck, scrambled up into the bed, and started going through that trash like midget buzz saws. Rosie made me sit over on the ice chest, and she sat down beside me on the old piece of an oxcart. She fanned me to cool off the sweat and to keep away the flies that swarmed around my garbage-stinking arms. She hummed a song, one of their songs, soft to herself. She held the stick in her other hand, slapping it up against her thigh every once in a while.

"Kramer, what happened to you? You look a little bad, a little ragged around the edges, a little filthy and unmilitary. In fact, you look a whole lot more like somebody that ought to be doing extra duty instead of somebody that performs important, classified duties. Maybe I ought to put your name back on that extra-duty roster."

"No, Sarge, don't do that. I know I look bad, but I can't help it. Your buddy, the spook, the high and mighty Mr. Gartley, decided that he wanted our garbage examined out there—examined in detail. He appointed me as the Head Examiner of the Garbage. I been slopping through that stuff in the backs of those trucks all day long."

"Well, that's good training for you. I'd do what he wants you to, though, if I was you. And try not to let the old man see you looking like that, garbage all over you and stinking even worse than you normally do."

"No, Sarge, I won't look like this no more. I got the solution to the problem all worked out."

"Yeah, OK, Kramer, but watch your step with the man. And remember what I told you about no shooting."

"Yeah, Sarge."

The next morning I woke up happy, thinking about Rosie. I put on a set of clean, starched jungle fatigues that I'd been saving for a run into Saigon after payday. It wasn't until I was in the jeep going out to work that I noticed I didn't have my stick. But then I remembered I'd left it with her yesterday. I'd even let her fool around with my pistol for a little while, and we'd played around and had a good time. I was really looking forward to a good day out there with Rosie.

"Good morning, Kramer, baby. You very handsome this morning."

"Yeah, Rosie, I know. I always was this good looking. You just never did see me for what I was. You got Fireball and the rest of them ready to go?"

Rosie would have made a good First Sergeant the way she strutted around, pointing at Fireball and his buddies with my stick and jabbering at them a mile a minute. She organized another four-kid team to back up the first team for the busy times when we had a whole lot of trucks waiting in line. I noticed that some of the special goodies from out of the garbage, like cans of food or C-rations or old jungle boots, were being taken out of the trucks by the kids and stacked up beside Rosie's ice chest. But that didn't matter. The kids were having fun, the truckdrivers were happy, I was happy, and Rosie was on top of the world.

"Kramer, what in the world is going on out here? What are those children doing on those trucks?"

"Good morning, Mr. Gartley. They're getting paper, sir."

"Oh."

"It's a pretty good system, Mr. Gartley. I thought of it yesterday after you left. It works faster, and we get more paper than the way we was doing it yesterday."

"Yes, it does seem that you've got quite a lot of it there."

"Well, yes, sir, but most of that's what we got yesterday."

"Yesterday! You mean to tell me that you left it out here last night, Kramer?"

"Yes sir. You didn't say to do anything with it, except to get it off the trucks. So I guess we did leave it out here last night. But we did pile it up there all together."

"Yes, I see, Kramer. Very neat. But we have to burn it, Kramer—destroy it. We do not want the enemy to have access to that paper. I suggest that we—that *you*—get started burning it right away."

"Is it all right if I get PFC Jones to help me do the burning?"

"It most certainly is *not*. Jones is my driver. He has nothing whatsoever to do with your operation here." Jones smiled at me from the jeep and turned back to his funny book.

All right. That was all right. I didn't mind burning the paper, and I didn't mind doing it by myself. It was a whole lot better doing that than playing in that garbage in the backs of those trucks like yesterday. I always did like a fire anyway, and I would have enjoyed this one, too, except for it being so hot already and for having to hear Gartley and Rosie talking back behind my back where they thought I couldn't hear them. I didn't like that too much.

"What you want, Mr. Four Eyes, baby?"

"I want to talk with you, Rosie. Just a little business talk is all."

"OK, business talk. You talk, I listen. No sweat."

"Not here, Rosie. That fool Kramer is right over there."

"Huh! I think you not want business talk. I think you want love talk!"

"Same thing, Rosie. Love talk, business talk all the same thing."

"Sure, same same. I know same same, Mr. Four Eyes, baby."

I heard them talking and laughing. It didn't matter to me. I didn't care what they did. They could have done whatever it was that they were going to do right out there in front of me, and I wouldn't have cared. But pretty soon they got up and walked in front of one of the trucks. They walked on across the road on to a path that led through some trees to a house, or rather what used to be a house before it got shelled by some of our artillery. I saw Rosie was in front and was leading that four-eyed idiot by the hand—and him carrying my stick like it was his. And I heard them laughing even after I couldn't see them any more.

I had figured that Rosie and me would be out there at that garbage dump for a long time. And we got along pretty good up until now—up until he started coming out here. I guessed we'd still get along pretty good. No reason why we shouldn't. But it wasn't going to be like it was before. Fireball and his boys brought over another big load of paper, and we put that on the fire and watched it blaze up hot so that we had to back off from it to keep from getting burnt.

I heard him yelling for Jones and me. We took off for the house at the same time, but Jones got there before I did because he was closer to it than I was to start with. I got in the door just in time to see Rosie cut a long, quick slash down the front of Jones's fatigue jacket. Jones jumped back from her like somebody had hit him. Rosie was laughing, and she had a straight razor in her right hand and my stick in her left hand. Gartley was naked, backed up in a corner, facing Rosie, and trying to cover himself up with his hands. I saw a slight thread of a red line running across both his thighs and another across his belly. Little drops of blood oozed out of the cuts, but I could see they were just scratches. Jones stood perfectly still, backed up against the wall beside Gartley, with his eyes on that razor blade of Rosie's. There wasn't any blood coming from the slash Rosie gave him; I guessed she hadn't meant to do anything except to scare him. And she sure had done that. She'd done a good job on Gartley, too. He was shivering like a man with fever and chills.

"Kramer, please, get that razor blade away from that woman. She tricked me into taking off my clothes, and then she tried to kill me with that razor blade."

Rosie laughed at him and looked over at me. I could tell that she was really proud of herself. "Rosie not kill, Kramer, baby. Rosie just want to cut off little souvenir from Mr. Four Eyes." She faked a slash at him. Gartley shrank himself up into as small a space as he could. He looked so pitiful naked and trying to protect himself with his hands that I almost felt sorry for him. Jones kept his eyes on the razor and said, "Corporal, you grab her from behind, and I'll get her hand."

I didn't move. Rosie looked over at me like she was trying to tell me something. Then I took three steps and stood right close beside her. She faked a slash at Gartley and another one at Jones to keep them backed up tight. She looked at me again. She sliced a button off my fatigue jacket quick as a snake striking. I didn't move. I knew she wouldn't cut me. I reached over and took the straight razor out of her hand. That's what she wanted me to do. She laughed at me so pretty, I almost forgot about Gartley and Jones being in there. She handed me my stick, too, and we turned around and walked out of that old house together. She started chattering about what an old fool old Four Eyes was, and after we got far enough away from the house for them not to be able to hear us, I started laughing about it, too.

It must have taken Gartley about ten minutes to get dressed and get his nerves back. Finally he and Jones came out of the house and across the road to where Rosie and I were talking. We hushed when they came out. It looked like Gartley wasn't going to take what she did to him as a joke. They came over to us and didn't say a word. Jones reached out for Rosie's arm, but she jerked it away from him just in time. He wasn't quick enough to catch her by himself, and he knew it.

"Wait a minute," I said. "What's going on, Mr. Gartley? What are you going to do to her?" I felt my heart beating faster now than it had when I took the razor blade away from Rosie. I could feel the blood pumping in my temples.

"We're going to have to take her to the village police, Kramer. They will probably do a routine questioning of her. You see, she is a threat to our security, and she is also engaged in blackmarketing. Under the circumstances, however, I have decided that it is better to handle this matter through the local police channels. Now you help us get her into the jeep, Kramer."

I thought about that for a minute. I was pretty excited, and I kept feeling like something terrible was about to happen. But I decided it would be better for Rosie to give in to Gartley now instead of causing a big fuss and maybe getting herself hurt or in bigger trouble than she was already in.

"All right, Mr. Gartley. Let me talk with her by myself. You and your brave PFC stay right here, and I'll explain the whole thing to her. She'll go with you if I tell her to."

I walked over to Rosie and touched her hand and smiled at her. I told her how it was, and she listened to me. I told her they were not going to hurt her but just going to turn her over to the village police. Everything would be all right. She would be with her own people. They would let her go today or tomorrow, and she could come back out here as soon as Gartley stopped coming. She started to cry and said please not to make her go, said the village police would beat her and use her and keep her locked up just to make the Americans happy. I told her that everything would be all right and that I would see that nobody hurt her. She looked at me so miserable that I almost started crying myself. But she said all right, she would go with them if I wanted her to. I took her by the arm gently and led her back over to Gartley and Jones.

"Very good, Kramer. I hope you talked some sense into this woman's head."

Gartley took my place beside her. Jones took her arm on the other side, and they led her toward the jeep. I could feel the blood beating in my head now, and my arms and legs felt dead and heavy. I wished I was dead. Knothead came over behind her and grabbed onto the seat of Rosie's pants with her little baby hand and followed along behind them. Rosie looked over her shoulder at me, and when she did that, she tripped and jerked her arm out of Gartley's hand so she could catch herself. Gartley must have thought she was trying to get away because he grabbed her shoulder and jerked her up straight and slapped her twice with his right hand hard, first with the palm and then backhanded. I saw Jones grin, and I saw his fist punch down hard into the small of Rosie's back, and she went down on her hands and knees. That wasn't enough for Jones. He took her hair in his fist and raised her head up to the right level and smashed his knee into her face. She went down quick. Knothead squatted down beside Rosie, crying and choking. Blood came from Rosie's nose and mouth and teeth, but her lips were moving, whispering soft to Knothead. The little girl got quiet and listened to Rosie.

In my head it felt like fire was spilling out of my temples and burning my forehead and eyes and ears and mouth. I leveled the pistol down on Jones and took the slack out of the trigger before I ever even thought about what I was going to do. Then I thought about it, and it made me glad. I took a deep breath. I was glad I was going to be able to kill him, so that I felt like singing when I squeezed the trigger.

click

It took just a second to figure out what had happened. I looked and saw the clip of ammunition had been taken out of the pistol. Rosie must have done that yesterday when she was playing around with my pistol. I lowered it and started walking toward them.

Knothead got up from beside Rosie with Rosie giving her just a gentle push. Knothead looked up at me and started walking. She walked through the crowd of old people and children and girls, and she talked to them low in her baby's voice while she was with them. She stopped and looked at Rosie once, and Rosie motioned to her to keep on going. The crowd of people was still at first, watching Gartley and Jones and me and Rosie. Rosie watched them go. Knothead led them to the edge and then down the hill across the road and finally down into that garbage pit. They all went, moving slowly, mournfully, down into that stinking mess, following that little girl.

"Kramer, you will do what I tell you, or you will stand court-martial for attempted murder. Do you understand?"

"Yes sir."

"You will get those people out of that garbage dump, and then you will help PFC Jones to secure this woman into the jeep so that she can put up no further resistance. Do you understand that, Kramer?"

I saw Rosie watching me on the ground with blood coming slower now, just a little from the corner of her mouth. She tried to smile at me. I felt it break, and then I felt it all spill out of me. And there wasn't any fire left in me to burn.

"Yes sir."

I took my stick, and I went down into that pit after those people.

They transferred me to another outfit where I got a pretty good job as a truckdriver, taking a deuce-and-a-half down to Saigon and back on the regular run with the convoys. I liked that truck, liked to feel that loud-winding engine in my hands and feet and belly. Sometimes I tried to remember how it was that day, and I remembered those thick glasses of Gartley's. And Rosie lying curled on the ground and looking clear at me. Then, if I pushed it, I could remember hitting, how it felt in my arm to hit them. The faces of those people down there don't come back to me—except for Knothead. But I can see a shoulder, or a back, or a knee, or an elbow. And I can see my hand with the stick coming down to hit. I can feel the hitting. But the worst is when I can remember feeling the muscle in my leg draw up and push down hard, and I can see my boot catch and stomp her leg down, and I feel the snap of it giving, and I see that baby bone flip up out of the flesh of her leg—and blood—and Knothead scream—I hear that scream tearing out of her. That scream is all I can hear. The rest is silence, even though I can still see them running from me and falling and me hitting and stinking garbage flying everywhere. I don't hear anything else after Knothead's scream. Just silence. I know they must have cried, too, but I can't remember any of the sounds, just the silence. And Rosie. I remember Rosie, still looking at me, even after I broke Knothead's leg, watching me do what I did.

Once, a long time later, just before I went home, I saw her in Saigon. She wore one of their dresses, blue light-swirling around her ankles and high collared. I slowed down the truck to wave, but she wasn't watching the convoy. And she wouldn't have known it was me that was waving at her, but just a sweaty arm pushing a hand out of a truck window from a long way off. She walked

The Proofreader

I

People who love dogs must have given up on human beings, thought Carson Moore. Reasonable enough, considering the way human beings acted toward one another in New York City. Going down the steps on a stepladder, God to man to animals, those people who love dogs have got to the absolute bottom rung of it.

In the Chemical Bank that afternoon, Carson witnessed a kind-faced lady trying to convert two free-breasted hippy girls wearing purple, speckled T-shirts into loving Jesus while all three of them stood in line waiting to cash checks. This lady had with her an old shaggy, brown dog, fat and full of love. The dog liked Carson. It stood up with its front paws resting on Carson's leg and panted up at him in a cheerful way. Walking out of the Chemical Bank onto the swarming hot Broadway sidewalk, Carson revised his thesis to read, people who love dogs also love God, but they do not care a damn for human beings. This suited him, and he decided to let it go at that. He turned his mind to the unleashed breasts of young girls and found the subject soothing as he walked upstream on Broadway toward the liquor store at 107th Street.

Carson Moore was a proofreader. He worked freelance, when he was in the mood. He didn't need the money because his wife worked as a ticket seller at the Thalia Theatre on 95th Street. For several years Carson had been bothered by his wife's talking to him whenever she was home. Six months ago Carson had silenced her by putting four ounces of Gilbey's Gin into his clam chowder every day at lunch. On the basis of this and other evidence, Mrs. Moore decided that Carson was crazy—harmless, but not someone she wanted to talk with. Besides, he had never listened to her properly, nor answered her with any sense. She did not miss talking to Carson. She continued to live with him, to take care of him more or less. She enjoyed keeping an eye on him.

If the weather was decent, Carson could usually be found sitting on a bench in Riverside Park near the 103rd Street steps. Here it was that he thought about love. It was a subject that severely troubled him. For weeks now, underneath his thoughts he had had this massive, rumbling doubt, that there was no love among human beings, animals, or in God. Only in books.

In the fall the weather turned cold, and the wind from off the Hudson River filled the park with swirls of brown and golden leaves. These days Carson liked best of all, certainly better than this hot, polluted summer. In the fall Carson would sit shivering happily on his bench with the lapels of his thick wool suit jacket pulled up around his neck to keep warm. His winter suit was a brown herringbone that he had bought at Brooks Brothers when he first came to New York more than ten years ago.

Carson was not yet forty, but he found himself remembering things the way old people did. He had decided that he felt much warmer toward older people than he did towards the damnably itching young. He had a certain knowledge of the older people in the park. There was a pale-faced man who wore a golf hat and who owned the friendly black dog named Mittens. There was a brisk German lady with a dog she called Heidi. And there was Vivien, frail, lonely, pulled all over the park by old Pal, a sour-tempered mutt that Carson would not have tolerated for a minute. Carson nodded to them, sometimes greeted them aloud. Most of them kept to a schedule, so Carson could predict their comings and goings. What was there to judge people by but their habits?

But Carson was fascinated by the young ones. They were the ones he watched most closely. He admitted it was an unhealthy kind of hunger.

One boy had taken to finding Carson at his bench every

day and talking to him. The boy smelled bad, wore glasses; he was silly and nervous with an annoying way of laughing at things Carson said. The boy owned a peculiar-tempered German shepherd that constantly ran away. When the boy whistled and called for the dog, his noise grated in Carson's ears. Carson did not like the dog, which whined a great deal and seemed always to want something. The boy talked to Carson about the Telephone Company. He explained to Carson an extremely complicated quarrel; with much relish he would tell about the various insulting things he had said to the business representative of the Telephone Company. The boy kept laughing in his hollow way, though Carson never smiled. Carson gathered that many people in the city did not like the Telephone Company, a surprise because he had always been fond of his telephone. Whenever it rang, which was seldom, Carson felt a little jolt of pleasure.

"You've lost all hope," Carson told the boy one day. "Don't you believe that a telephone call might sometime change your life entirely?" Carson himself believed this still, though in more than thirty years of telephone calls, not one had changed his life. Nor had the postman done him any good.

The boy had laughed as though Carson had said something funny, and it hurt Carson's feelings. It was this sort of thing that made Carson swear never to talk about anything that he cared about with anybody he did not fully trust. Even talking with his wife was better than being kicked in the tender parts by strangers.

Carson entered the liquor store at Broadway and 107th Street; immediately he was comforted by the full shelves of bottles. Carson had never explained to anyone his delight at being inside a liquor store. He strolled from one end of the store to the other, his hands behind his back, occasionally taking a bottle down from the shelf to examine the label or look at the price or just feel the thing in his hand. The man behind the counter did not question Carson. When Carson had finished his tour of the store, he bought the same things he always did, two sample bottles of Gilbey's Gin. These he would take to the park for sipping during the hot morning. The counter in the store was old-fashioned, made of thick wood, worn now to a light, grainy brown, which Carson liked to run his hand over lightly while he waited for his change.

On 107th Street there were Puerto Rican children whom Carson enjoyed watching while they played. They were used to seeing him pass this way and so continued their game as though they were not being watched. An older woman with a rag tied around her hair sat near them to keep them out of the street when cars came. Once in the park Carson had his money taken from him by three teen-aged Puerto Rican boys. He had lost only eight dollars, but the boys with their knives had scared him. And they had called him "motherfucker," which shocked him. The word "motherfucker" had stayed in his mind for days afterwards. It amused him now, though, a word with a comical sound to it. He tried to roll it off his tongue to himself, the way the Puerto Rican boys had done, but he couldn't make it sound the same. It was a funny word, even the way he said it with his southern accent.

Settling onto his bench, Carson began to gather up the threads of his thoughts on love. He took off the light-blue pinstripe suit jacket, seven years old now, that he wore in the summer. He folded it carefully across the back of the wooden park bench. Then he uncapped one of the little bottles of gin and drank half of it. Spatters of sunlight played over him, shining through the tree leaves above the bench. A breeze coming off the Hudson cooled him pleasantly. He watched the Circle Line Tour Boat, painted white and green with a handsome red trim; it went south along the river. Carson wished for an instant that he himself were on that boat, smelling the water, looking across at Manhattan Island and Riverside Park, perhaps even catching a glimpse of the man sitting alone up there in the shade. He promised himself that he would sometime take that Circle Line Boat.

If there were such a thing as love among the creatures of the earth, Carson could know about it only if he had some of it himself. He set about trying to find love in his own heart, and it was difficult. For one thing, he could not tell the difference between what was a permanent feeling inside himself and what was just something temporary that would pass away and be gone the next time he looked for it. For another thing, he had trouble figuring out how he felt about Mrs. Moore.

Most of what Carson liked about his wife was remembering the way she used to be before they were married. She was a Virginia girl, slender then, almost coltish. She'd gone to a rich women's college where there were willow trees, acres of grass, brick buildings with white columns. Something sweet caused Carson to catch his breath, the memory of his trying to take off her panties in a hillside graveyard on a hot summer night fifteen years ago. He had not been successful, but the try had been a real pleasure to him. Now Mrs. Moore was like a polar bear, sluggish, sloppy, with flesh sagging all across her hips and her belly. At home she drank quarts of beer straight out of the bottle, belching as though Carson had no ears. It made Carson cringe to think about her talk. It had been an unbearable sourness to Carson when she continually harped on the bitchery of her girlfriends, coworkers, and neighbors. Still she could be very kind to him, even now, when she had stopped talking to him. She took a special care in ironing his oxford-cloth shirts. Probably she was still proud of him, as she had been in their first years in New York, though now she certainly should know better. Absent-mindedly he wondered what degree of failure it would take before she stopped being proud of him.

Carson Moore had come to New York to be a poet. Why in the hell did people think they had to come to New York to be something they could just as well be, with half as much trouble, in New Mexico or Iowa or Georgia? Nevertheless, they did come: sculptors, painters, actors, singers, musicians, novelists, dancers, and damnable poets. He was tempted to put these reflections about artists into some kind of comfortable statement about America and art in general, but decided against it. He went back to the more solid ground of thinking about himself and his poetry.

Poetry, like sex, was a damnation. Carson had, in the bottom of his chest of drawers, buried under a mound of long underwear that he refused to wear, a manuscript of

237 unpublished poems; each one had cost him much tedious crafting to get it exactly right. It was not correct to say that he was unpublished. He had, in fact, published three poems, one in *The Georgia Review*, another in *The Red Clay Reader*, and a third, his biggest success, on the editorial page of the Sunday *New York Times* of February 15, 1962. Carson had made $43.00 with his poetry. He had close to two hundred rejection slips; these he had burned on the day he swore off poetry. It wasn't that no one understood his verses; it was simply that he wrote mediocre poetry and couldn't stop himself from it, though in the past five years he had managed to prevent himself from putting it on paper. Even this he did not trust; he suspected he was merely storing up poems in his mind that he would some day put down on paper in an absolute fit of poetry writing, all of it mediocre. Worse, he could not bear his wife's bringing out old copies to show people. The poems, all 240 of them, the published and the unpublished, Carson felt to be an embarrassing expression of his own stupidity, foolishness, and damnable awkwardness of emotion.

A squirrel scrambling down the side of a tree clung upside down for an instant while examining Carson, flapped its tail twice as though to register Carson, and dropped to the ground, ignoring him. Carson had no special feeling for squirrels one way or the other. His hunger was for human beings.

In a split second the squirrel scrambled back up the side of the tree, just missed by a large, rust-colored dog that knocked up dirt and leaves when it skidded to a stop at the base of the tree. The dog, a young Irish setter, crouched at the bottom of the tree with every muscle stretched tight, straining to look upward. It ran twice around the tree, jumping up on its hind legs and barking with a ridiculous coon-dog kind of yelp. This tickled Carson. He admired the way the animal's ears flapped outward from its head and the graceful hairy places at its tail, chest, and legs. He saw its owner coming toward him, a girl dressed in white, with pretty legs.

"That's a beautiful animal," said Carson. The girl had long black hair the texture of a horse's tail. She was thin, had a good face in Carson's judgment, and she wore no makeup.

"He's a disgrace," said the girl. She sat down on the bench beside Carson, a yard and a half of wooden space between them. "Come here, Zee," she called. The dog ignored her and continued to bark, standing with its front paws propped up against the tree. The squirrel was gone. Carson noticed that the girl was not wearing a brassiere, and this pleased him.

"Gin," Carson told the girl, showing her the bottle. He felt in the back of his throat that it was time for another sip, and he wanted the girl to know exactly what was what. The only other young person Carson had talked with in five years or so had been the bad-smelling young boy with glasses and a grievance against the Telephone Company. Carson was not at all sure how a person went about talking to a young girl like this with pretty legs and no brassiere. He knew he preferred to watch young people, but he didn't know if he wanted to talk with them. If that boy had managed to hurt his feelings by merely laughing at something he said, a girl like this might have the power to put him into a permanent state of despair. He noticed that she was hot from walking; there was a line of perspiration above her lip.

"No, thank you," she said quite pleasantly. Something about her reminded Carson of a younger Mrs. Moore, perhaps the slender, lightly-tanned legs. Carson thought about panties and how one went about trying to get them off a girl's hips in a graveyard at midnight.

"Zee, come here!" The girl stamped her foot on the cement walk in front of the bench to show the animal that she meant business. The dog came immediately this time, slackening its ears and wriggling up to the bench in exaggerated humility. It sat down, smelled the girl's knee, and then began to lick it, swabbing with its pink tongue. Then it put a large, filthy paw on the girl's leg, smearing black mud on her. "Zarathustra!" shouted the girl at the dog. She stood up.

This tickled Carson, who had some understanding of the ways of dogs, but he managed to keep his laughing to himself. "Is that really your dog's name?" he asked the girl. His attention was caught by the way her breasts jiggled when she brushed at the dirt spot on her knee.

"Do you have a handkerchief?" She purposely ignored his question. Carson dug in his back pocket and gave her his clean handkerchief. The girl took it, spat on it, and rubbed at the dirt spot on her leg with it. Then she sat down and handed the handkerchief back to him, making no effort to hide the fact that it was wet and dirty. "What is your name?" she asked him.

"Carson Moore," he told her. She seemed to take it in without particularly caring whether or not she remembered it. She patted Zarathustra's head to show that he was forgiven. Zarathustra trotted out onto the grassy area in front of them, sniffing the ground for squirrel scent. Carson watched a barge chugging north on the Hudson so slowly that it seemed not to be moving at all. He could think of nothing to say to the girl that might interest her. He looked at her hand resting on the bench, and he was touched by the slenderness of her fingers.

"Are you a musician?" he asked.

"No." She looked out toward the river, not giving him any attention. Carson decided to speak boldly.

"I'm a proofreader," he said. He decided to lie if necessary, though he disliked lying on purpose; he considered it bad enough having to lie as much as he did accidentally. "Right now," he said, scooting closer to the girl as he spoke, "right now, I'm reading the galleys for the new Paul Barnes novel." He watched her closely but saw no change in her expression. He uncapped the second bottle of gin and finished it. He decided to try the method of honesty on her.

"I come down here to the park to think about love." Carson decided to go no further, to remain silent until she replied. He watched the dog, now chewing a fallen tree branch. A breeze stirred the tree limbs and caused the speckles of sunlight to skitter pleasantly over the ground in front of them. Down on the concrete walk at the bottom of the park, Carson watched an elderly couple, the old man shuffling along in a rumpled gray suit and white straw hat, his wife, healthy-looking, bare-headed, with a ponderous bosom, strolling easily along with her arm at the old gentleman's elbow. Zarathustra perked his ears and stopped chewing to stare at a sparrow that lit not three feet from his large black nose. Carson could smell his own gin breath and wished for some mint-flavored chewing gum.

"What have you decided about love?" the girl asked, turning to him. Carson couldn't tell if her expression was one of amusement or interest. He watched her hand move a fraction of an inch closer to him on the bench. She wore a ring with an extremely large, oval brown stone; the ring completely covered the first joint of her finger.

Carson let a certain amount of silence pass before he replied. He made his voice sound solemn and truthful when he finally spoke. "Well, I have decided that there is no such thing as love, that what draws people together is chemistry,"—here he paused to let her figure out what "chemistry" meant—"and that what keeps people together, like that old couple there,"—Carson pointed to the elderly people moving slowly below them—"is just damn habit."

Without looking at him, the girl nodded, as though she were actually acknowledging something the Hudson River had said to her.

"What have you decided about sex?" asked the girl. The question plopped into Carson's brain like a rock in a mud puddle; it took him a minute to get his mind organized. The dog dropped its tree branch, scared the sparrow away, and came over to pee on the bench behind them.

"It is a damnation," said Carson finally. "It's like poetry and disease. It makes you do stupid things, regrettable things. It tangles you unbearably with people."

Carson wished he had another bottle of gin with him. He seemed to have used up all the energy that he might have got out of the two small bottles he had already drunk. The back of his throat itched for more. The girl smiled at him, showed him her even, white teeth. Carson's own teeth were yellow, a little bucked, and one of the front ones was angled sideways, so that he rarely smiled, even when he felt like it. Mrs. Moore's teeth, however, were even worse. She had a lead-gray cap on one of her eye-teeth that gave her a hard appearance like a woman wrestler.

"Don't you like orgasms?" asked the girl. Carson felt his head go dizzy inside. The girl didn't wait for him to answer. "I mean, I really like orgasms, and I just can't imagine why anyone would not like to have them," she said.

The word "orgasm" jangled in Carson's mind. He thought of that other word that amused him, "mother-fucker." He almost said it out loud but thought better of it. Carson watched the girl pull down at the skirt of her dress, a thin knit material that clung to her breasts and hips and stomach. He was certain now that it was her legs that reminded him of Mrs. Moore fifteen years ago. He wondered if this girl would become a polar bear, too. Also, he thought about her panties, and then he wondered if she would ever iron oxford-cloth shirts for some failure of a husband.

"Orgasms are nothing." Carson tried to say it as though he used the word all the time, but it came over his tongue queerly; he went on anyway. "They are just spurts of juice that last only a few seconds."

"Oh, no!" said the girl. She seemed earnest and ready to argue the point with Carson, who felt uncomfortable in this conversation anyway. "Orgasms go all over you. They last and last," she said. "Whenever I have an orgasm, I feel it tingle in my ears and all the way down in my feet. It's like it touches the very center of me. Also, they put me in a better mood for hours."

"I see," said Carson and crossed his legs. He felt a certain tingling himself and wondered what was going to come out of all this. He told himself to let this be a lesson and to keep his damn honesty to himself the next time he felt like informing somebody that the reason he came down to Riverside Park was to think about love. The words kept popping in his brain like ping-pong balls: Orgasm. Motherfucker. Orgasm. Motherfucker.

On the flat, grassy level of the park in front of them, a boy and a girl began playing Frisbee. They were both barefooted. The girl had a swatch of golden hair that al-

through the brown clouds of dust we threw up in the streets. Rosie was still pretty. I reached down for the gearshift to shift up into third, but my hand missed the stick so that I had to look away from Rosie a second to see what I was doing. When I looked back to the street, I had lost her.

that the action of slicing would distract him, but it didn't. He put down the lemon and headed for the door. It was hard for him to catch his breath. He thought he was certain to begin crying before he could get out of the door. The despair kept coming on him, harder. He wanted to die.

"Mr. Moore, where is my drink?"

His brain ricocheted.

Naked, Leslie seemed incredibly slight and fragile. She was tanned only a little, but the light-colored bikini outlines at her breasts and her hips and belly made that flesh seem especially vulnerable. Carson blinked his eyes to keep back the tears. A peculiar mass of feeling was pushing at him; this was sorrow, elation, loss, grief, fear, lust, anticipation, excitement—feelings mixed and confused even more by Leslie's being naked. He walked back into the kitchen and fetched her drink to her. She stood very straight, looking at him curiously, and took the drink like a small child accepting a glass of milk before bedtime. She thanked him and turned toward the room she had just come out of.

"Come and talk to me while I take a shower," she said. She took his hand and led him into the bedroom, impossibly junked up with clothes, dirty sheets, shoes, underwear, stockings, books, magazines, letters, records. Carson wondered if she actually slept in that bed buried with clutter. Leslie led him into the bathroom and put down the top of the commode. Carson sat down and took a good, solid sip of his drink.

The shower curtain was clear plastic with patterns of green, blue, and yellow circles in it. Carson could see every single bit of Leslie through it, his vision being dimmed only by the shower water splashing on her skin and making it shine. He concentrated on looking at the ice in his drink.

"I can't stand Paul Barnes," she yelled at him from inside the shower.

"What?"

"I said, I can't stand Paul Barnes," Leslie yelled again, louder this time. She peeked out at him through one of the green circles in the shower curtain. "His books make me depressed. Like the way you look, sitting there: depressed. I like cheerful things." She ducked back inside the shower and commenced to splash noisily. Carson continued to feel miserable. He thought he would go home in a minute and have his clam chowder. Afterwards he would take a nap.

"I was lying," he confessed to her. "I'm not proofreading the new Paul Barnes novel. The last thing I proofread was *Gang-Bang on Main Street* by Troy Greenberg." This was the truth. Carson had taken to working for the pornography publishers in hopes of brightening up his life, but pornography depressed him. He felt guilty in the presence of children whenever he had been reading pornography. *Gang-Bang on Main Street* had been a lousy book anyway.

"I can't hear you," Leslie said. She poked her head out around the shower curtain and grinned at him. Something about the way she looked, healthy as a girl in a television commercial, made Carson shiver. He was a thousand miles away from this girl, from his own wife, from everyone.

"I said, things are disintegrating. Everything is coming apart, and the only thing I really want to do is die!" The words came blurting out of Carson's mouth without having passed through his mind. He would have held them back, if he could have. Worse was that now he felt tears making his eyes salty. He began to cry, his lower lip trembling like a child's. He took a sip at his gin glass, but his throat would not perform the act of swallowing for him. "Shit," he said, and gave himself up to whatever it was that was making him want to cry. He wept while he sat on Leslie's toilet seat.

III

Leslie had a tendency to be too tender toward people, even absolute strangers sometimes, particularly if they had a vulnerable look about them like this Carson Moore. The tendency had caused her to get a mild beating up once by two soldiers she met when they asked her for directions in the 59th Street subway station. Leslie didn't quite understand why the two boys had wanted to hit her, because all she had done was invite them to have lunch with her, fix sandwiches for them, soup, crackers, cheese, and Pepsi-Cola. But then when they had finished eating, they had hit her. And even though they did it more or less half-heartedly, they had bruised her ribs and her cheekbones. They had taken her money, her rings and bracelets, including the charm bracelet that she had had since her freshman year in high school, and her watch. Then the boy she liked the best had gone through her record collection and taken fifteen albums. The other one had suggested that they might rape her, but his buddy, the record-stealer, had said no, that she would make too much noise. He had belched and winked at her and said that it was too much trouble. Leslie had been glad of that. She thought it was because the soldier felt sorry for her, crying, and her cheeks had been swollen then. It was stupid of them to hit her, she thought.

She stepped out of the shower to go and try to help Carson, slumped, blubbering on her commode, but dressed like a businessman in a light-blue suit. Poor, stupid, helpless people, she thought.

Wet, with her breasts goose bumped, cold from stepping out of the warm shower, Leslie went to Carson and folded her arms around his head. Now and then she patted him on the back and crooned to him, though she didn't know why she did any of these things. What possible good was it to give comfort to another person when he would likely turn out to be some kind of pervert or neurotic? Probably this one would turn out to be a real bastard. She held him close to her.

"Hush now, Mr. Moore," she said. She felt his tears against her belly, a kind of warm-water feeling. Looking down at the man's head resting against her stomach, Leslie was startled to realize that she was actually enjoying this whole painful scene. "Jesus Christ," she said softly to herself; she made herself sick sometimes. She looked up at the ceiling, still holding Carson, and tried to concentrate on good things, sunshine in the park, music, smoking grass with someone she liked . . .

Carson pushed her away from him, got up off the commode, and walked out of the bathroom.

"I don't know why the hell I'm crying and making a big fool out of myself," he said. Carson took the dirty handkerchief out of his pocket, shook it, and blew his nose. He tried to think of some way to call her attention to the dirt on it and to make her regret having soiled it.

"I know why you're upset," Leslie told him. It wasn't true; she didn't know at all, and she certainly thought it was peculiar of him to be acting this way. Nevertheless, she wanted to say something to help him. "Why don't you lie down on the bed and rest a minute. It'll make you feel better."

Leslie came into the bedroom and pushed the clutter off the bed onto the floor. There was only a bottom sheet, fairly filthy and gray-looking, but there was a good pillow with a pretty blue polka-dotted pillowcase. She fluffed up the pillow and put it at the top of the bed for him. "I have a very informal life-style," she told him and smiled at him as she went back toward the bathroom. She thought he must be feeling better now, and it gave her pleasure. More times than she could count, Leslie had found herself taking care of some boy or man, beginning with her brothers in high school, who had drunk too much liquor, got sick, and had to vomit. She'd always been loyal and stuck by those people, even though most of them hadn't appreciated it much.

Without taking off his suit jacket or his shoes, Carson lay down on the bed. He kept his body perfectly straight with arms at his sides, playing a game he had invented in the army, pretending that he was lying down in the position of attention. Like self-hypnosis, the game had helped him to go to sleep on narrow, sagging army bunks in crowded barracks when sleep had seemed impossible. Carson closed his eyes and let his mind swirl in slow whirlpool circles...

"What the god damn hell?" Carson jolted up to a sitting position to find Zarathustra standing over him and staring gloomily down into his face. The dog resented Carson's presence on the bed; it stood with its legs splayed and its ears drooping.

"You god damn beast! Get your Irish setter ass off of

this bed!" Carson told the animal. In Carson's view, dogs belonged outside. Zarathustra ignored him, went to the foot of the bed, walked in a circle twice, and curled himself up into a comfortable dog's position, his eyes still fastened balefully on Carson. Carson was about to say more to the dog, if necessary to use his foot to urge Zarathustra to get back down on the floor. But Leslie came back into the bedroom, saw the man and the animal eyeing each other, and began to laugh at them.

Carson was not amused. He put himself back into his rigid position, intending to ignore both Leslie and the dog. He closed his eyes, but could not get them to stay shut, and left a foggy slit of light between the lids. He could not keep from looking at Leslie. She didn't seem to care whether he looked at her or not. She dried herself with a yellow towel, her hair hanging around her shoulders, damp and tangled like a cave woman's. Fifteen years ago Carson had had the habit of pretending to keep his eyes closed so that he could watch what Mrs. Moore was doing without her knowing he was doing it. Mrs. Moore didn't care whether he looked or not, either, but Carson tried to be covert about things whenever he could.

A loud, weary sigh came from Zarathustra. The dog had laid himself out flat, all four legs stretched out away from himself, looking like a deer carcass.

"Comfortable, beast?" Carson mumbled.

"You leave him alone," Leslie told him. Carson said nothing, shut his eyes tight, and made himself as rigid as possible. In a short while, he felt the bed sag with Leslie's weight. He cracked his eyelids enough to see her sitting beside Zarathustra at the foot of the bed, facing Carson with her legs crossed Indian style. Still naked, she began brushing her hair.

"The trouble with people like you," she addressed the shut-eyed Carson, "is that you think too much about things. Love is something you do, and you don't have any choice about it. It's like the way your hair and your fingernails and your toenails grow, which are things you can't do anything about. But the way you are, you think and think about it until it seems like you don't love at all. You make it disappear by thinking about it so much. But everyone loves, whether they like it or not, even the ones like you."

"That's how come I got married to the silent polar bear," said Carson. "I didn't think." He still had an urge to kick the dog off the bed.

"That's a cruel thing to say." Leslie smacked him on the shin with her hairbrush. "You don't seem like such a prize yourself, you know."

Carson knew this was so, and he felt sorry he had spoken so badly about Mrs. Moore. The urge to confess came on him powerfully, and he sat up, with his head braced against the headboard of the bed, and looked directly at Leslie.

"You're not married; so you don't know how it is, but I'll tell you, all I see about my wife is that she's fat and getting old. And all she talks about are things that make me depressed. She doesn't talk to me any more. She doesn't care what I do, but we're still tied to each other like bad habits that are too much trouble for either one of us to break."

Carson took a close look at Leslie to see if she understood what he was talking about. She didn't look at him, sat staring at the dog beside her, absent-mindedly brushing her hair. Bars of sunlight from the bedroom window touched her and showed a light golden down on her arms and her thighs.

"What's worse," he said, "is the fact that I never made it as a poet, even though I worked hard at it. I managed to blame that on her. I used to have this theory that I couldn't write if I spent too much time around my wife. I claimed that a man had only a limited amount of creative energy, and if he spent too much of it with his wife, then he wouldn't have any left to use putting poems down on paper. So she liked to spend right much time with me back then, and I was always trying to get her to go somewhere else. I blamed the whole thing of my not being able to write decent poems on her."

Leslie was mad at him. She whacked him with the hairbrush a good bit harder than was necessary just to get his attention. Then she shook the brush at him while she talked in such a way that her breasts jiggled fiercely at him.

"Now wait a minute, Carson Moore! You act like you're the only person ever to have problems being married. You are such a baby! I'm sorry, I just don't have any sympathy for you." Leslie began vigorously rubbing the dog, which was laid out flat beside her.

"I know, I know," Carson said. "I don't feel sorry for me either." He sat up, hugged himself, and rocked back and forth, squeezing at his guilt, trying to rock it out of himself. "It gets still worse, though. See, I kept on writing these poems even though I knew they weren't any good. I made myself write sonnets and sestinas just because it was a discipline I could put myself through to force something down on paper. It was terrible. I wrote sonnets about masturbating, and nobody wanted to read poems like that. I sent these miserable poems out to all kinds of magazines, and all I got was one rejection slip after another. But I knew the god damn poems were going to be rejected. I would have rejected them myself, if I had been an editor." Carson paused to take a sip of his gin. He was beginning to enjoy the sordidness of the confession.

"I did it to worry her," he said solemnly. "Every time I got a rejection slip, I would show it to her, and I'd say, 'I got this poem here rejected.' And I'd kind of shuffle my feet around and look down at the floor like I'd tried my best and failed. Then she'd try to comfort me, you know; she would come over and put her hand on my shoulder, or give me a hug, and she'd tell me not to worry about it, to send the poem somewhere else. Sometimes she'd sit down and read the poem carefully, studying it, you know. And she might ask me a question or two about the thing. Anyway she always acted like it was a hell of a fine poem and like she didn't understand how those clods could possibly have rejected such a masterpiece. I'd act like I was listening to what she was saying. Then I'd indicate to her that she just didn't understand the poem. Like she didn't understand me and she didn't understand my poetry, and there just wasn't any hope for her because I was a god damn artist!" Here Carson shouted to get a better effect.

"See, what I was doing with every one of those rejected

poems was like taking a razor blade so sharp she couldn't even feel it and cutting her with it, just a little at a time. That's evil. I know it is. And I don't even know if I knew exactly what I was doing to her when I did it. The full understanding of what I was actually up to came to me at a later time, after I had already sworn off poetry, which, incidentally, I blamed on her, too. That was the final thing. I had all these poems, and all these rejection slips, and one day, I got myself worked up into a high state of emotion, and I said to her, 'I can't go on.'" Carson paused a moment. "I told her, 'I just can't write poetry and be married to you.' That was what really did get her. It was like I finally killed whatever it was in her that I had been working at all that time."

Leslie stared at him. "Is that all?" she asked.

Carson hugged himself tighter. "No, not quite. See, I convinced her that she was responsible for the ruination of my creative genius and for the waste of my life. So now I had the right to do anything I wanted to. And I decided to entertain myself. She already had a job at the Thalia Theatre, which she was supposed to quit whenever I got to a certain point of success. Obviously that time never did come, and I guess I didn't really want it to come. So I gave her to understand that she could keep the job permanently. Ordinarily that wouldn't have suited her even a little bit because she had a college degree and could have got a whole lot better job than that if she had been thinking about a career. But she just accepted it because she felt guilty about what she had done to me. Since she had destroyed me, she was responsible for keeping me alive. She accepted it.

"That left me free to do whatever I wanted to, which was to spend my time down on Broadway and 42nd Street and 8th Avenue, places like that. I am a known customer in every peep-show joint, every pornography shop, every theatre that shows filthy movies, every strip joint and go-go house in this town. I can even get discounts in some of those places, I've been such a regular customer. I buried myself in that stuff, wallowed in it. All those people down there on Broadway that you see on the street, I know them. I'm one of them."

Carson had got to the point now where he wasn't sounding like he was sorry about things; instead he sounded proud of himself, almost bragging.

Leslie got up off the bed and went to her dresser. She took out a brassiere and a pair of panties and slipped them on quickly. Then she left the room.

"Wait," Carson called after her. "I'm not finished."

"Don't bother," she yelled from another room. He could hear her bare feet marching over the floor, going somewhere.

"Come here, Zee," she called to the dog from what sounded like the kitchen. Carson could hear water running. Zarathustra woke up and stood up on the bed, shook himself, looked at Carson, and yawned a big toothy kind of Irish setter yawn. He stepped over Carson and jumped off the bed to go find Leslie. In a second Carson heard Leslie's bare feet padding back toward the bedroom. He looked at the door just in time to see her come in with a large cooking kettle. Two steps from the bed she stopped, took aim, and drenched him with the kettlefull of cold water. The shock was severe to Carson. "You no good son of a bitch!" Leslie said. Then she threw the empty kettle at him.

IV

They walked uphill on 103rd Street toward West End Avenue, Leslie marching ahead of Carson, who was bedraggled and soaking wet. Carson could tell by the way she walked, with a brisk snap, pop of her hips that Leslie was still mad at him and wasn't about to stop being mad for a while. He thought he ought to be up walking beside her, but he didn't want to, and so he lagged back. He had looked at himself in the mirror after she splashed him; he knew he looked like a half-drowned pelican.

Leslie had told him before they left her apartment that they were going together to see his wife. Carson damn sure didn't want to do that, but then again, he thought, maybe it would brighten things up somehow. He watched her skirt swish, swash back and forth up ahead of him. He thought about her naked buttocks, wihch he had been able to look at just as much as he wanted a few minutes ago; only he hadn't really looked then because it made him too nervous. Now that he couldn't see, he wanted to. It is certainly some kind of terrible, incurable disease that I have got, he thought. He wondered what Mrs. Moore was going to have to say.

"Hard-headed, water-throwing bitch," he said entirely to himself. Still he followed her. Still he dripped.

When they got to the corner, Leslie stopped and waited for him to show her which way to go. She looked at him hard, like a mother does at a child who has messed his pants. Carson thought about turning the opposite way from where he lived. He was thoroughly capable of doing such a thing, and other kinds of trickery besides, but he decided not to. With the limited knowledge he had acquired about Leslie, he figured she was the kind of a girl who would sock the devil out of him right there on West End Avenue, if she felt like it. He turned the corner and went into his own building, opened the downstairs door for her, and led her up the stairs to the first floor where he and Mrs. Moore had lived ever since they had come to New York. Carson rang the door bell to give the polar bear time to get herself ready for whoever might be at the door. He and Leslie stood waiting.

The door opened, and there she was, big as the state of Texas, holding a half-drunk bottle of Miller High Life in one hand and the doorhandle in the other. Mrs. Moore had on an old, ripped, greyish-colored slip, and her hair frizzed out at all angles. It pained Carson to look at her face, which was puffy like a big piece of cauliflower.

The way Mrs. Moore stared at Leslie, she might have been seeing Greta Garbo or Ingrid Bergman, her favorite movie stars. She didn't even notice how ridiculous and wet Carson looked. Leslie stared back at the older woman for a couple of moments. Then she took Mrs. Moore in her arms and began to cry softly. "You poor girl," Leslie said. Mrs. Moore was surprised, but she accepted the sympathy. It had been quite a long time since she had been able to do any decent crying, the last time being when *Anna Karenina* showed at the Thalia Theatre a year ago; Mrs.

Moore had sneaked out of the ticket booth to see Garbo throw herself under the train. Mrs. Moore began to cry with Leslie. They patted each other on the back like sisters.

"You poor girl," Leslie said again.

"Oh, shit," said Carson. He went to the refrigerator where he kept his gin, poured himself a drink, and put it down his throat fast. Then he went to put on dry clothes.

V

"I want to talk about your husband, Annie," Leslie said after they sat down together on the sofa. Leslie had asked Mrs. Moore what her first name was, and Mrs. Moore had told her, even though she was accustomed to being called Mrs. Moore by almost everyone. Nobody at the Thalia where she worked knew what her first name was. But it made her feel a little younger to be called Annie, and Leslie was so pretty, seemed like such a sweet girl, that she didn't mind.

"Yes, well, he's worth talking about all right," said Mrs. Moore. She suspected that Carson had done some outrageous thing to Leslie, and this didn't surprise her. It would have been a perfectly logical extension of Carson's increasingly peculiar behavior over the past few years. She wished he would go back to writing poetry. Carson was in the kitchen rattling pots. Leslie called in to him, "Be quiet, Carson." Then she spoke to Mrs. Moore. "I don't know how you've managed to live with him all this time, Annie."

Mrs. Moore was curious to find out what Carson had done to Leslie, but now she felt the need to defend him, or to defend herself for having married him and stayed with him. She felt at least two different ways about him. On the one hand he was peculiar, a little crazy, and certainly worthless. On the other hand he was sensitive, decent, and wonderfully independent. Whenever she made up her mind to be objective about Carson, something came up to confuse all her thinking. Like this attack of

Leslie's against him. At such a time Mrs. Moore committed herself to one or another viewpoint, and allowed herself to be totally unreasonable.

"No, honey," she said, "it hasn't been bad. I mean it hasn't been as bad as you might think from just looking at the way he is now." Saying this made her think of the way Carson had been when he came calling for her at her dormitory before they were married. He had been such a bright-looking person that it was hard to be around him without getting into a good mood. His eyes and his mouth made him look like he was always about to smile or to laugh. He had been one of the best-dressed young men she had ever known, his suits always perfectly pressed, his shirt starched, and his ties exactly the right color. He had walked very straight then, confidently like a rich young lawyer. The other girls in her dormitory had made a production of drooling and cooing over him whenever he came to visit Annie. This had delighted Carson, made him preen and prance in front of them and charm them with his elaborately good manners. He had not been a shy person, but a gentle one, a quiet person.

"It's been good, actually, now that I think about it," said Mrs. Moore. She got up and went to the kitchen where Carson was rummaging around in a cabinet under the sink, looking for something. Mrs. Moore wanted to touch his back, wanted for the first time in months to speak to him, but she didn't. She thought it was best to check your feelings and see if they lasted from hour to hour, or day to day, or week to week, before you did anything. She took a glass from a cabinet and poured the rest of a bottle of beer into it. She returned to the living room without saying anything to Carson. She did notice that he had changed clothes, that now his suit was an old grey one.

"But, Annie, he told me the things he did! He was horrible to you." Leslie looked like she was about to start crying again.

"Listen," Mrs. Moore told her gently, "what Carson Moore says and the actual truth about things are two entirely separate things. They are usually not much closer than ten miles apart. When he's talking about himself, he can't any more tell the truth than he can fly. I don't mean that he sits down and thinks up a pack of lies to tell people. It's just that he can't see himself. He can talk about himself all day long, not tell one single true thing, and still believe that he's being absolutely honest." Mrs. Moore settled back into a corner of the sofa, getting herself comfortable. It was a long time since she had been able to talk freely with anybody, and she liked Leslie.

Carson came into the living room. He sat down in a chair across from Leslie and Mrs. Moore and began to examine his shoes. He felt considerably better now that he he had on dry clothes, though the pants of this old suit did not fit him.

"He's above average in being peculiar. Now even I will admit that, and it's sometimes embarrassing to me to be married to him. I don't know whether you have noticed it or not," said Mrs. Moore, "but Carson Moore is the type of a person who likes to watch people and think about them and talk about them and so on. But he can't stand to get himself involved with anybody. He'd rather jump into a pot of something nasty than to talk to some bum or panhandler on the street. What's funny is that they always know the way he is just from looking at him, and they seek him out because they know he'll give them money to keep from having to talk to them. He's like that with his old friends, too, especially the ones he knew in the army. He likes to know about them, all about what kind of job they've got and who they married and how many children they have. But he can't stand to have one of his old buddies come to visit him. He can't stand to talk on the telephone either, for more than two or three minutes at a time."

Carson got up from his chair and went back to the kitchen. He was careful not to make so much noise that he couldn't hear what Mrs. Moore was saying about him. She ignored him and continued telling Leslie about his characteristics.

"So anyway when he got this announcement in the mail that they were going to have his high school class reunion, I naturally decided that Carson would not want to attend. I couldn't imagine his getting himself involved with all those people he used to know in high school and having to talk with them and meet their wives and their children. For about a week he didn't say too much about the reunion, and then one night he mentioned to me that he had sent in a money order to pay for us if we decided to go.

"Now Carson went to high school in Lebanon, North Carolina, and I don't know about you, but I had no special desire to spend a weekend in Lebanon, North Carolina. I would rather stay in New York and work, because at least that way I get to see the show at the Thalia. But Carson wanted to go. I suggested he go without me, but he wouldn't do it. He said that I had to go and take care of him in case he got too nervous talking to all his old buddies or in case he got to drinking too much. Finally I said all right. We stayed at the Howard Johnson's Motel, which wasn't bad. I like motels, especially if I have a good stack of magazines with me to read while I'm there.

"Next morning Carson was nervous as a convict. He went out and got himself some breakfast. Then he came back to the room where I was trying to get some sleep. Then he went out again to get coffee and read the paper. Then he came back in again. It was about nine o'clock, and I don't ever get out of bed until after eleven, even when I'm home. I felt like slugging him in the mouth."

Carson came out of the kitchen, carrying a tray with a bowl of clam chowder and some soda crackers on it. He carried it to his chair to sit and listen. He began softly blowing on the chowder to cool it. He could tell from looking at Leslie that she was impatient, that she wanted to interrupt Mrs. Moore. But he knew his wife was going to continue. He had heard parts of this tale before; it always interested him to hear Mrs. Moore talk about him. He thought she seemed most intelligent when she was talking about him to other people; sometimes she even said miraculously true things about him that he had never thought about. He hoped Leslie would be able to endure it all. He swore to himself that the next time he was alone with Leslie, he would do something or say something so dramatic, so decisive that she would instantly love him. Mrs. Moore went on.

"The first thing on the list for the reunion was this

picnic at the John Carr Memorial Park, a mile or two from the motel. Carson was ready to go at one o'clock, and the picnic didn't start until three. I was wide awake at that time because Mr. Ants-in-His-Pants there was walking around in circles in the motel room, blowing his nose, going to the bathroom every five minutes, and so on. But I was not going to any picnic two hours early. I stayed in bed and read my magazines until three o'clock exactly. Then I got up and dressed to go to the picnic. Carson was so nervous by that time that he couldn't think straight.

"There was a bunch of his old cronies standing around the parking lot drinking beer out of cans, probably the same thing they did all through high school. Well, the first thing they did was have a big laugh over how long Carson's hair was, because at that time Carson was going through a phase of not getting his hair cut. They had a big laugh about his hair and his being a beatnik and so on. Carson got so self-conscious he couldn't even say hello. It didn't matter, because they just slapped him on the back, and one of them went over to the trunk of his car and got a beer for Carson. Then Carson rattled off a big batch of nonsense about New York and North Carolina and how the two places were more or less different from each other. He didn't make the slightest bit of sense, but everybody laughed, and they slapped him on the back some more, and some of them said 'good old Carson.' Apparently Carson had been peculiar in high school, too, and so they expected him to act that way at the reunion.

"Now one of the things you will learn about Carson is that he is very perceptive about other people, and he can be very intelligent in some awkward situations if he wants to. He figured out that everybody there expected him to act peculiar, and that was what he did the entire afternoon. He introduced me to this gawky friend of his, who had lived next door to Carson and who had gone to school with Carson ever since the second grade; Puckett was what this person was called. He was a skinny man with big elbows and rotten teeth. Carson and Puckett started talking about all the killings that had occurred in the Lebanon area. A good friend of theirs, a classmate, had shot his brother, which seemed to tickle Carson and

Puckett. Another good friend of theirs had jumped on a man's back and cut the man's throat; Puckett and Carson dwelt on that event for a good twenty-five or thirty minutes, going over the way people said the man's blood looked on the ground, and how long they said he laid out there before the ambulance came, and so on. This seemed to have been the central event of their boyhood, but then they started talking about Puckett's uncle who had got into an argument with a man named Phoenix Jones, and Phoenix Jones had got an ax and sneaked up behind Puckett's uncle and split the uncle's head square down the center with the ax. Puckett's uncle had lain out in the woods for hours before a man found him and slung him up on a mule and took him home to his wife with his head split wide open. Puckett's uncle wasn't killed because the ax had gone right down between the two halves of his brain, not damaging either side much, except that he had a slight paralysis of his right arm and leg. I was impressed with him, I'll tell you.

"So then Carson got together with another old friend of his, with whom he had played in a hillbilly dance band in high school. Carson and this character started singing these ridiculous songs in two-part harmony, except that neither one of them could sing or remember the words. But they had a good time annoying the devil out of everybody. People would walk by and say things about Carson's hair, and he would shake it out for them, cross his eyes, and make himself look like some kind of a wild man.

"An old girlfriend of his came up and told him that he was just as good-looking as he ever was. Carson stuttered and spewed about how she was still pretty herself, too. Except she wasn't. She was one of those very boney type of women. The older they get the more makeup they wear. But she acted like she was Miss Sexpot of Lebanon, North Carolina, which maybe she was for all I know. Carson never even introduced me to this girl, whom I didn't really care to meet anyway, but he took her down to the creek bridge in the park there. I could see them, Carson picking at a stick and throwing little chunks of it into the creek and her wiggling around like a sixteen-year-old. I am glad to say that the girl's husband put an end to that episode before it led to any further embarrassment for anybody. The husband went down to the creek bridge and joined them. I heard him start talking to them in a loud voice, and it wasn't but a few minutes before they came on back up the hill, the three of them. Carson came over and grabbed on to me like he hadn't seen me for days. While he was amusing himself with Puckett, his buddy from the hillbilly band, and his boney old girlfriend, I was supposed to be entertaining myself without his assistance among this group of people who were absolute strangers to me. I was having a marvelous time, and I told him so, told him exactly how I felt about the whole show. It did not faze him. Carson was so full of himself that day that it would have taken a shotgun blast to have any real effect on him.

"The men started playing horseshoes, because evidently that is a very popular pastime in Lebanon, North Carolina, and, of course, Carson had to get into it. He started dancing back and forth between the two posts while the people were trying to play and kind of cheering them on. He and Puckett took off their shirts because they got hot with all that exercise. They looked like undernourished apes. They were not the type of men who ought to have been putting their bodies on display. Instead of being disgusted with such an exhibition, his classmates thought it was marvelous. They thought that was the way people from New York ought to act and they certainly thought it was appropriate behavior for Carson. His old boney girlfriend got loose from her husband again and came and watched, standing right up close to the horseshoes game. She giggled and snickered and clapped her hands. I myself could have died of embarrassment right on the spot. I wanted to go back to Howard Johnson's and read my magazines until it was time to drive back to New York. But I had no way to go, except to walk, which I was not about to do.

"The worst thing was just before they ate. They asked Carson to say grace over the potato salad, hot dogs, hamburgers, cole slaw, and deviled eggs. Carson launched himself into a thing that I cannot describe to you, some kind of a semireligious spiel of thirteen-syllable words about God and love and man and animals. It went on for twenty minutes before somebody had the good sense to yell out 'Amen!' Carson shut up then just like he had planned to end the thing at that point. What he said didn't make a bit more sense than if he had been reading words out of a dictionary. But I'll swear, Leslie, four different people, including the old girlfriend, came up after we finished eating and complimented Carson. You would have thought that he had delivered the Sermon on the Mount.

"I did finally get Carson away from the picnic by telling him that we absolutely had to get back to the Howard Johnson's for me to get ready for the dance at the Lebanon Country Club. I tried to relax myself at the motel by taking a nice hot bath and by reading a magazine, but Carson followed me all over the room, even into the bathroom, jabbering about how great it was to be back there in Lebanon with Puckett and his old buddies and how Lebanon was his real home, where his 'roots' were, and how he never should have moved to New York, and so on. I asked him if he considered his old girlfriend one of his 'roots,' but Carson ignored that. He talked about how he could get a good job there, teaching in the Lebanon High School, and how it would be a good thing for both of us to get the hell out of New York. We could settle down and live in a house with a front yard like normal people, and he could write some decent poetry.

"See, at that time, Carson had the habit of bringing up the subject of his poetry whenever there was something that he especially wanted or didn't want to do. Now he knew that I knew he was full of baloney when he used his poetry as an argument for doing something like moving to Lebanon, North Carolina, since it had been because of his poetry we moved to New York. But he also knew I wouldn't argue with him about it for fear of really hurting his feelings. I don't claim to know anything about poetry, but one thing I do know is that Carson always had this tendency to feel guilty about writing it, like it wasn't really worth doing and like he ought to have been selling insurance or building houses or picking up garbage, anything as long as it was honest work. So you have to be very careful not to say anything to indicate that you think poetry is not the most serious and necessary project in creation.

"You would think that everybody in the whole United States of America knew the difference between a good poem and a bad one from the way Carson used to act about it. It was a mistake even to hint to him that nobody gave a damn. But all that is neither here nor there. What I did in the Howard Johnson's was agree with Carson that maybe it would be a good idea if we moved to Lebanon. I suggested maybe it would be good for him to go and drive around and look for a nice place for us to live. He took my suggestion and left immediately, which allowed me a good hour's nap before he came back talking about the places he had looked at, as if he had looked all over town. He tried to make it look accidental that he had met Puckett in a beer-drinking place. He'd brought Puckett back to the motel with him, so I didn't say anything. I ended up driving the car out to the Lebanon Country Club with Carson and Puckett drunk as coots in the back seat, reminiscing about another killing."

Mrs. Moore took the last sip of her beer out of the glass and went to the kitchen for a refill. Leslie didn't speak to Carson in her absence, and Carson kept his silence. He looked intently at the empty clam chowder bowl.

"Well," said Mrs. Moore as she sat back down on the sofa with a full glass of beer, "when we entered the Lebanon Country Club, I could feel the change. Carson and Puckett didn't feel anything at all. But it was like everybody had grown porcupine quills during the time between the dance and the picnic. The lights were turned down and there were two couples dancing to an old record they used to play when Carson's class was in high school. But it wasn't working. Everybody acted unfriendly like they just resented the devil out of being taken back to the good old days. They were all sitting around these tables with white tablecloths on them, and everybody was drinking as fast as they could put it down. You could feel little waves of hostility passing back and forth, like the people at this table would be talking about somebody at that table and the ones behind them would be making some comments about a person on the other side. It was just so sad I wanted to turn around, walk out the door, and go back to New York. But no indeed. Carson and Puckett jumped right into the thing like everybody had just been waiting for them. Those two started to holler and laugh and slap people on the back. And they had this game of going around to the various tables and picking up other people's drinks and taking sips; except their sips were big swallows. Some people thought it was funny and others didn't, but it didn't make any difference to Carson and Puckett. And the character who had played in the band with Carson joined in. Well, they were having just a splendid time, and there I was, standing right inside the door where Carson had left me without taking the trouble to find me a place to sit, and I could tell the whole inside of the country club was about to explode, but Carson and Puckett and the other one were not about to stop. I was really a little scared. I'd never seen Carson act like that. It was like he had reverted to his high-school self, except that the obnoxiousness of his character was intensified ten times by being old and drunk.

"Then I noticed the old girlfriend sitting at a table with her husband, staring at Carson with her eyeballs glittering, like he was the biggest hero ever to hit town. I'll swear she looked adoringly at the man, and at the time he was making a complete, total, absolute ass out of himself. He must have been evoking old memories in her mind or something. But he was certainly evoking something else in the husband's mind besides old memories. I could tell that from all the way across the room. The husband had on a winter suit that looked hot to me, and his shirt collar must have been a size too small because his neck looked pinched and his face was red. Carson, even if he didn't have his normal wits about him, had enough judgment to stay away from that table, but Puckett didn't. Carson tried to stop him at the last minute, but he wasn't fast enough. Puckett pranced right up to the old girlfriend's table and let out a loud, goofy laugh. The girlfriend gave a little giggle. Puckett bent down, put his arm around her boney old shoulder, and took a big, long, lingering swallow of her drink. When he did it, the husband got up from the table and walked over to Carson and knocked him flat.

"If you know anything at all about Carson, you know he takes things philosophically; that is, he always exaggerates the meaning of everything. That's what he did in this case, and the incident made a deeper impact on him because nobody went to help him. Puckett and the buddy from the hillbilly band didn't want to incite the husband any further, and the old girlfriend lost interest in him after her husband floored him. I, of course, was still boiling mad at him, and I did not respond as fast as I might have in other circumstances. So Carson laid there a little while without anybody paying any attention. Somebody played 'Rose, Rose, I Love You' on the record player, and a couple got up to dance. The girlfriend's husband went to the men's room to wash his hands. Carson just laid there on the floor by himself.

"After a little while I did go over and help him get up. He wasn't hurt except for being a little sore in his right jaw, but you would have thought he had just barely survived a major beating. He made me take him outside to the golf course and made me listen to him while he ranted and raved. Puckett came out and tried to cheer him up, but Carson wouldn't have it. He went on and on about how Thomas Wolfe was one hundred per cent correct, you can't go home again; and how it was a damn dreary, hideous world when the people a person loved from his childhood turned on him and hated him; and how he never should have left New York to come down to this god damn hick town, Lebanon, North Carolina, where people hadn't even learned the first rules of civilization and so on. Then he said that he and I were going to leave, but he made me go back inside with him and dance with him once just to show those primitive sons of bitches in there that they had not got him down in the slightest. And we did that. Carson danced like a corpse, but with his jaw stuck out in defiance and so on. I was so glad to get back to the Howard Johnson's I didn't even try to explain to him how everything would have been just fine if he had acted halfway normal."

Mrs. Moore hushed and sighed and let Leslie consider for herself the evidence of Carson's idiosyncrasies. Carson went to the kitchen with his tray.

"After we got back to New York, I wanted to talk with Carson about his high school reunion," Mrs. Moore continued. "I wanted to discuss it and get the thing out of both our systems, but he wouldn't have anything to do with even talking about it, like it never happened. What I wanted to tell him was that even if he was a little unusual compared to those people in Lebanon, I still preferred him. I did tell him, but I don't know if it had any effect. After that he went through his phase of giving up poetry entirely."

"Yes, he told me about that," Leslie told Mrs. Moore. "He tried to blame you for the fact that he couldn't write anything decent. The bastard! He said he almost destroyed you by making you think it was your fault. He said it did something permanent to you."

"Well, he says that sometimes," said Mrs. Moore. "I'm beginning to think he believes it, he says it so much. But he knows it isn't so."

Both Leslie and Mrs. Moore looked over at Carson sitting again in the chair, but he said nothing to them. He looked blank, as though he had not been listening. Mrs. Moore went on.

"I know part of the reason Carson tells people that big lie about blaming me for his giving up his poetry is that he has this craving to explain to himself why he and I are getting old. He can't stand to look at me and see me ugly and fat and wrinkled and hard. You can't really blame him. It makes me sad to see myself this way, too, but I take it better than him. I think Carson has been afraid of getting old ever since he was in his twenties. When he sees me like this, it reminds him that he is just as old as I am. Well, he can't bear to accept it. Carson has to have a literary kind of explanation. He wants something dramatic to explain why I am the way I am and why he is the way he is."

Carson cleared his throat, though he continued to examine his shoes. Mrs. Moore glanced at him for an instant.

"Yes, damn him! He's right. He knows when I'm off

track. I used to talk that way about his god damn poetry whenever he and I had been fighting or drinking. Sometimes we would stay up all night yelling at each other. I know I'm wrong when I get to talking like that. It just makes me sad that he wants me to be as pretty and fresh and young as I was when I was a college girl. And there isn't any way in the world that I can be that way again. . ."

Mrs. Moore was about to cry. She meant to hold it back. Leslie took her arm and patted and said, "You poor girl."

"Shit," said Carson.

VI

They stood at the door while Leslie said goodbye to Mrs. Moore. "Goodbye, Annie," she said.

"Goodbye," said Mrs. Moore. She still wore the ripped slip, and her hair still frizzed out, but now there was a kindness in her expression. The talk had done her good, and Carson could recognize a certain familiar softening in her attitude. All of a sudden she remembered something.

"Wait," she said. She let the door shut just a second, not actually closed, but with the latch open and holding the door open a fraction of an inch. They heard Mrs. Moore rummaging somewhere inside in what sounded like the drawer of a desk or a bureau.

"Here," she said when she opened the door again. "Take this with you." She handed out a sample bottle of Gilbey's Gin.

Carson reached and took it, even though he was not prepared for such a thing. He could think of nothing to say. The door to the apartment shut, and the latch clicked.

"She spoke to you, you know," Leslie told Carson as they passed through the downstairs door onto West End Avenue. Carson did not reply; he considered his wife's act closely. Inside his pants pocket he held the sample gin bottle in the palm of his hand.

West End Avenue was bright with the midafternoon sun. Neighborhood people were outside warming themselves, chatting with each other, watching other people. The Puerto Rican lady who was the superintendent of Carson's building nodded to him in a friendly way. Young women with grocery carts, laundry carts, or baby carriages passed back and forth across the avenue, heading for Riverside Drive or for Broadway. In a wheelchair in front of a building across the street sat an old man with whom Carson had an argument two years ago. The old man's name was Mr. Calahan, and the argument had lasted about a week, Carson and Mr. Calahan shouting at each other every day on the street. Neighborhood people had watched them and listened to them and generally savored the argument, but now neither of the two men spoke to each other. Carson still had the urge occasionally to go over there and shout at old Calahan; he had thought of a good many excellent things to say, and it irked him not to be able to use these remarks. To Carson's surprise, Leslie waved to the old man. It was a good enough wave, certainly a cheerful one, but old Calahan across the street did not wave back.

"He's a nearsighted old bugger," Carson told her.

"He is not an old bugger," Leslie said, "and how would you know if he's nearsighted or not?"

"I used to talk with him every now and then until I found out how narrow-minded he was," Carson replied. It was certainly true that old Calahan was nearsighted; his glasses were a good quarter of an inch thick; they made his eyes look buglike from close up.

"I like him. He gave me a plastic rainhat the other day, and he always speaks to me very courteously," Leslie said.

"I see," said Carson. Privately he was convinced that old Calahan in his wheelchair was a lecher and entertained nothing but filthy thoughts all day long.

"He is also very nice to the children around here," Leslie informed him. His opinion of old Calahan stayed fixed, as it had been for two years.

They turned the corner and walked down 103rd Street toward Broadway. Beginning at the Cairo Hotel, midway down the block, a line of garbage cans, some with lids but most without, stretched along the outside of the sidewalk all the way down to the Geneva Hotel at the corner. Here the air stunk intensely. In front of a shiny new Mustang squatted a burnt car with all four wheels gone and all its windows broken out. From a window three floors up in the Geneva, music came beating down to the people on the sidewalk, a celebration, "The King Is Dead."

Sitting on the iron railings at either side of the hotel entrance was a group of people chatting, laughing, and drinking beer from cans and bottles in brown paper bags. It reminded Carson of a large country family outside, having a good time. A woman slouched against a car. A man had his pants legs pulled up to cool his swollen ankles. In a chair with no back to it sat a big-stomached man with his eyes glazed, his mouth partially open; he seemed about to fall off the chair onto the sidewalk. Leslie tapped him lightly on the knee as she walked past him, and the man's eyes flicked open.

"Wake up," she called back to the man and smiled at him.

"Right, darling," said the man in a funny, deep voice that sounded muffled as though he might have been speaking through a wad of old newspapers. There were guffaws from some of the other men back closer to the hotel; then there was a tight silence while they listened to something another man said. A louder burst of laughter followed the remark, and Carson was sure that all of it was directed at Leslie and him.

They stood beside each other and waited for the light to change for them to cross Broadway, heading east. Carson looked at Leslie and nodded his head in the direction of the Geneva which they had just passed.

"Squalor," he told her.

"Yes," Leslie said, "maybe so."

They walked through a housing project for old people, large brick buildings of maybe twenty stories, concrete sidewalks, and small plots of grass. Then they crossed Columbus Avenue into another housing project, this one for black people and Puerto Ricans, and it seemed the same as the one for old people, except here there were children. They went through the project to Manhattan Avenue and downhill toward Central Park. On this block buildings were old and cluttered; the street was littered with garbage; people sat outside on the front stoops of the buildings. Here the traffic had been cut off, and a volleyball net was strung up. Young black people were playing a good, hard game of volleyball, and Carson was surprised to see two black girls playing on each side, all four of them quite pretty. As Carson and Leslie walked past the game, he watched the girls and saw that they played with the same quiet seriousness as the boys. Only once did he hear any of the players laugh. The ball, knocked out of bounds, came toward Carson, and he caught it and threw it back, feeling a kind of exhilaration in the quick move it took to throw the ball. He was surprised to see that the ball went generally toward the player he had intended it for.

"Hey, you're a volleyball player," Leslie said to him, teasing.

"Obviously," said Carson. He was pleased that she had remarked the thing he did, and he took a ridiculous, heart-pounding pride in having caught and thrown back the volleyball. At Central Park West they turned left, uptown.

At 106th Street there were steps leading up a hill into Central Park. The hill was steep, and Carson was afraid he would be exhausted before they got to the top.

At the top of the hill there was a large flat area, a playground filled, it seemed to Carson, with several thousand black and Puerto Rican children. Almost all of these children wore clean white T-shirts with some lettering on them. Carson concentrated on one shirt that seemed to be standing still for a second and saw "PPP" stenciled on it.

"What is PPP?" he asked.

"People's Park Program," said Leslie. "It's to keep the kids off the street, hopefully away from the pusher and out of trouble. Mostly it just means we come up here and play with them for three hours in the afternoon. You'll enjoy it," she told him cheerfully.

Carson thought to himself that there was too god damn much life in this area. The playground seethed with children moving in all directions, and it resounded with a constant shrill noise like that of bees' wings in a hive. Some of the children saw Leslie. A mob of them ran toward Leslie and Carson. "Leslie, Leslie, Leslie!" they called.

"Good God!" said Carson aloud. Carson was scared to death of children. He had devoted a major portion of his life to avoiding them.

Surrounded by a throng of vibrating, shouting, small people, Leslie swept into the play area like a long-awaited queen accompanied into her court by her subjects. She turned her head briefly to tell Carson something he couldn't hear for all the noise.

Then Carson was alone and separate among all the children in that part of the park. He considered leaving the park entirely and perhaps walking back toward West End Avenue. But he knew if he did, he probably would not see Leslie again.

He watched two small boys playing a game, which after a moment he realized was a modified version of basketball. Instead of a hoop ten feet off the ground, the boys were using a large, screen-wire trash can for a basket. The ball they used appeared to be standard size, and they played on a concrete area in front of a small brick utility building. When Carson got close, one of the boys slapped the ball away from the other boy. The ball came toward Carson, and he stopped it to keep the boys from having to run after it. He handed the ball to the larger of the two boys, who had reached him first. The boy's expression was one of extreme irritation with Carson.

"Aw, man, shit! What did you stop the ball for?"

"God damn, man!" registered the small boy in full agreement with the larger one.

Carson did not know what to do or say, and so he did nothing and said nothing. The larger boy handed the ball to the smaller one, who began dribbling toward the waste can. They went quickly away from Carson, not concerned with him any further, as they would not have been concerned with a stone wall or a rock or a tree. Carson could not keep himself from watching the two children play their game. Neither of the boys could have been more than eleven years old, and yet they played with a

dead seriousness and expertise that seemed to Carson
unnatural. One boy's offensive fakes and shots and moves
would be almost perfectly matched by the other boy's de-
fensive alertness and quickness, the same as Carson had
seen in professional athletes. And a certain etiquette
seemed to be in effect so that they rarely argued about a
point, or whether such and such a thing was fair, or
whether one of them had cheated; rather, they seemed to
be in harmony about things and to be in absolute concentration on the game. Carson remembered that his own
childhood games, mostly baseball because of living in a
small town in the country, had been characterized by a
high degree of argument and debate; one's ability to
bluster and complain and curse was taken as part of one's
overall athletic value. Carson had not been a good athlete,
but he had been good at arguing, and the seriousness of
these two black children playing an improvised game of
basketball troubled him. He noticed that he was the only
person watching the two boys play, among hundreds of
children and several adults in the area. Carson thought
that he should have gone somewhere else, but he was
fascinated with the game, and he couldn't make himself
get away from it. The boys kept score, and Carson per-
ceived that the smaller child was ahead by several points.
When they reached thirty, the game stopped with the
small boy grinning because he had won.

"Man, you can't beat Earl Manigault," the small boy
told the large one. They walked in circles around the
waste can, cooling off. "You just not good enough, Albert."

"Shit, you just lucky. You ain't Earl Manigault, and you
ain't never gonna be Earl Manigault," said Albert, full
of contempt even though he had lost. "Come on, let's
play one more game," Albert said.

"I'm ready," said the small boy and grinned while he
dribbled the ball on the concrete. He passed it casually
behind his back and up again, bouncing it between his
feet.

A tall young man came over to Albert and the small
boy; he was about eighteen, and Carson assumed he was a
counselor in the People's Park Program.

"O.K., Earl Manigault, let's go." Albert gave a very

cocky appearance when he addressed the small boy. The counselor tossed the ball up into the air, and the game began immediately. Albert scored two quick points, and looked to Carson to be a formidable ballplayer, moving with a certain confidence that seemed to overwhelm the small boy.

"Hey, Earl!" Albert mocked the small boy. "Hey, Earl, don't cry now." He shut up when the small boy faked and went in for an easy lay-up point in the trash basket.

Carson walked over to the counselor and asked, "Who is Earl Manigault?" The young man looked at him briefly and then looked back at the game in front of them. For a long moment he held his silence, and Carson wondered if he should repeat his question. The young man stood with his arms crossed in front of him, a muscle twitching near his shoulder, and the silence stretched.

"Earl Manigault is a junkie. He's in prison for getting caught robbing a store."

"I see," said Carson. He did not understand.

The counselor nodded his head toward the boys playing ball. "Earl was a ballplayer before he went to jail. He was a beautiful ballplayer." The counselor paused and then added quietly, "Maybe the best there ever was."

"I see," said Carson. "I'm sorry. For whom did he play?"

The counselor smiled at him and said, "Earl didn't play for anybody. He played up there." The counselor pointed north. "Earl played mostly at 135th Street."

"I see," said Carson.

"No, you don't see," said the young man. "Quit saying you see. You never did see one of those games up there, or else you'd know who they talking about when they say Earl Manigault. They talking about something you never have seen, Harlem basketball, man, street ballplayers! Earl Manigault was a better ballplayer than anybody you'll ever see. So is Joe Hammond and Helicopter Knowings and Connie Hawkins. But you don't know who I'm talking about, man; it's something you don't know anything about."

Carson was quiet. He felt hot in his ears and at the back of his neck. He wished he hadn't said anything to the young man standing beside him now. He wanted to move away because he imagined that he could actually, physically feel the counselor's anger like heat from a fire while he stood beside him. The two boys went on with their game. Albert was staying ahead of the small boy, but the small boy kept up the pressure, trying desperately to win. The counselor spoke again to the proofreader, this time in a gentler tone of voice.

"Those two there are going to be street ballplayers, a lot of boys up there are." The young man pointed north again. "They start playing when they're a whole lot younger than these two here." The young man stopped and let Carson savor what he had said. Then he went on.

"Dope and basketball. They got it up there, man. You ought to go up there some time and have a look at it."

The ball was knocked upward, went high into the air and came over to where Carson and the young man stood beside each other. This time Carson was fully alert and did not try to stop the ball from going past them. The counselor, however, put his toe in the place where the ball came down and caused the thing to jump into his hands. From there it flicked upward again into the air as though it had made one smooth, perfectly graceful curve up off the ground and back up toward the waste can. The ball hit the can as square and final and absolute as the period at the end of a sentence.

"Shit, man, what did you do that for?" Albert asked the counselor. The young man did not reply, but walked away, leaving Carson alone to watch the game.

VII

Albert won the ball game. He beat the small boy, and then he laughed at him. The small one was tired, and he had tried hard to win. So he went over to a tree by himself and cried.

The proofreader went to find Leslie, wishing Albert had been the one to lose.

A concrete circle like a racetrack bordered the playground. Around this circle children were furiously riding bicycles, taking turns on the rickety vehicles that PPP provided for their use. A PPP counselor directed the riding, decided what child would ride when and for how long; he stood with the children waiting in line under a tree. On the track bicycles raced along as fast as the children could pump them. Carson had to pick up his feet and trot to keep from being run over by boys on bicycles. They yelled, "Beep, Beep, Beep!" at him as he crossed the track, and he felt foolish trying to move so fast. He thought one boy actually swerved toward him to try to brush him.

Carson had seen Leslie on the other side of the playground, standing with a group of children lined up to take turns riding a horse. Light-brown with a black mane, the horse plodded around a small circle of grass to the side of the concrete. Here the land was rocky, and there were trees farther down the side of the hill. As he got closer Carson saw Leslie helping a small girl with pigtails up onto the horse's back. The animal was so tall that the child sat several inches above Leslie's head. The little girl whimpered at first, frightened by the height and by the closeness of the animal; she was a frail Puerto Rican child, about nine years old, dressed in a T-shirt and blue jeans. Leslie grinned up at her, comforted her, and told her to sit up straight in the saddle.

Carson did not know what scared the horse. Just as he came up to the group of children, he saw the horse's head flick sideways. Then it jerked away from Leslie and trotted away with the child clinging to the saddle but lurching backward and forward with the movement of the horse. The little girl seemed pitiably small on the back of the huge animal.

"Hold on, Renata! Hold on!" Leslie yelled at the little girl and began to run after the horse, her skirt flapping high as she ran.

Carson stood and looked. He was terrified for the child but uncertain that he could do anything to stop whatever was going to happen.

A swarm of children and counselors began moving across the playground after the horse and the child, but Leslie ran faster than anyone. Only Carson stood still, ashamed of himself for not running but unable to make himself act. He felt the hot afternoon sun beat down on his head and shoulders while he watched. He thought about leaving the playground, getting away from whatever terror was coming. He could not even make himself do that, so he focused his eyes and his mind on the child, Renata, bobbing up and down and getting farther and farther away from him.

The horse stopped trotting, lowered its head, and began to eat the scrub grass that grew around the rocks on the hillside. In that instant Leslie caught up and snatched the child off the animal's back and ran off a few steps, holding Renata in her arms. The horse continued to munch the scrub grass.

Carson stood and watched Leslie, carrying the child in her arms, come toward him; the crowd of children and counselors followed behind her.

"Carson, can you carry her?" Leslie asked him.

Carson took the weeping child in his arms and patted her back. The child clung to him. Immediately he stopped being afraid of the little girl. The child was not heavy, and he could feel the heat coming from her frail body. Renata sobbed quietly against his shoulder. Carson looked at Leslie and saw a shiver pass through her even though the sun was shining directly on them.

"I didn't do anything," he said to her. "I just stood there. I didn't run."

"I know you didn't," Leslie said, and she touched his coat sleeve. "You think too much. And, of course, I don't think at all. It's hard to say which one of us is worse."

They walked a short ways, and then Leslie asked the child, "Renata, do you think you can walk, sweetheart?" Renata stopped crying, but she kept her head buried in Carson's shoulder.

"No," said the child; her voice was muffled in Carson's suit coat.

"Well, I can carry her now, Carson," Leslie offered.

He answered quickly. "No, it's all right, I can do it. Where are we taking her?"

"Home to her mother."

They walked out of the park, following a path of concrete that wound through trees and brush, a gradual slope down the side of the playground hill. As they walked, they were sprinkled with afternoon sunlight. Renata lifted her head off Carson's shoulder and looked him level in the face while he carried her. She examined him closely and gravely, without speaking to him. He could smell her breath, a sour-sweet, chewing-gum child-smell that touched a deep memory of Carson's.

"Does she speak English?" Carson asked.

"Of course she does."

But he could think of nothing to say to her.

They came out of Central Park at 100th Street and walked uptown on Central Park West to 103rd Street. When they turned west onto the street, the little girl spoke to Carson for the first time, though she had been looking directly at him for several minutes. She surprised him with the exactness of her speech.

"Let me down, please."

Carson put the little girl down on the sidewalk. She held onto one of his hands and kept holding onto it as they walked along. Halfway up the block a small boy in shorts and a PPP T-shirt came out of an apartment building and ran to meet them. The boy's hair was cut close to his head, and the skin of his legs and face was a darker brown color than Renata's.

"That's Joseph, Renata's younger brother," Leslie told Carson. She spoke to the little boy in a scolding tone of voice. "Joseph, why weren't you in the park today?"

Joseph simply grinned up at Leslie and took her hand, the same as his sister had taken Carson's hand. Renata began to chatter to the boy in Spanish and to gesture at Leslie and Carson. This surprised Carson, too, the sound of her speaking rapid, staccato Spanish. Carson couldn't understand any of it. He supposed that Renata had told her brother about her experience with the horse.

"She go for a ride, huh?" Joseph asked Leslie, grinning, gleeful. Carson saw that the boy thought it was splendid his sister had almost fallen off the horse.

"Yes, Joseph. She went for a ride. She was a brave girl. She was much braver than you would have been with that horse, Joseph," Leslie told him.

"Bullshit," Joseph said. Renata kicked at him, but she missed. She kept holding Carson's hand.

They came to the building, and Leslie said goodbye to Renata and Joseph. Renata let go of his hand and went to Leslie. "Wait," she said.

The child pulled Leslie's arm, and when Leslie bent down, Renata kissed her. Then she went back to Carson, pulled on his arm, and made him bend down to her. She kissed his cheek with a touch so quick and fragile that Carson thought for an instant he might have imagined it. No, it had happened, he was certain of it. Then Renata ran up onto the stoop of the building and hit her brother a good sock on the shoulder. Joseph hit her back, and they began wrestling and giggling.

"Goodbye," Leslie called to them.

Carson stayed silent while they walked uphill toward Manhattan Avenue. It was late afternoon and still warm. The street had a comfortable smell to it, a city-asphalt smell that Carson suddenly realized he liked very much.

VIII

Heading west on 103rd Street, Carson and Leslie walked deep in the shadows of the apartment houses. The late afternoon sunlight rinsed across the tops of the buildings, coloring them a bright orange. Once, and then twice, a window high above them caught the sun and sent a shaft of light splitting down into the shadows where they walked. They went slowly, easily, without talking.

Crossing Columus Avenue, Carson tried to think how he felt about that child who had kissed him. She would forget him tomorrow, or the next day, or the day after that. But how was he supposed to describe, even in the privacy of his mind, that quick, piercing feeling toward her? And what had made her kiss him? Not love, but it wasn't not-love either.

He walked beside Leslie, coming toward Amsterdam Avenue now, where cars sped north too fast to be registered by the eyes or the mind. His feet moved in a sort of dance with hers, and he shuffled to get himself in step with her, as he had learned to get in step with his platoon in the army. He thought about Leslie naked, and he wondered if that meant anything.

Across Amsterdam Avenue, going downhill toward Broadway, he saw the 103rd Street subway station, the welfare hotels, the small Puerto Rican grocery store where he did his shopping, the shoe-repair shop, the German candy store, the Japanese Koto Restaurant, the Discount Drugstore. . .

"Broadway always reminds me of an orgasm," Leslie told him.

"What? What did you say?"

"I said that all these people flowing back and forth across and over and in and out of Broadway make me think of an orgasm," she told him.

"I don't quite see the connection," Carson said, which was a lie, because he did see what she was talking about.

As they tried to cross Broadway, a mass of people began pouring out of the subway station. Carson and Leslie found themselves being bumped and battered by people on all sides. "Excuse me, excuse me," Carson said; it was a habit of his to excuse himself to people, even though he thought most people in the city did not bother to say excuse me. Leslie moved ahead of him in the crowd, looked back, and giggled at his trouble getting around a fat, Irish-looking lady.

By now the sun had passed down below the level of the buildings. Only the top of an old hotel on the corner of 98th Street had the orange color of warm sunlight. The city had become cooler, and Carson, cold-natured as usual, felt a chill pass through him.

When they finally got across both lanes of traffic on Broadway, Leslie saw someone and pointed in the direction of downtown.

"There goes Annie Moore," Leslie told him; she was excited and she pushed at his shoulder. "If you hurry, you can catch up with her."

Sure enough, there she did walk, Annie Moore, wearing a light-yellow dress and heading downtown at an easy pace, her hips wide and her back held straight. In that dusky moment on Broadway she appeared like a sailing ship passing out and away from a crowded harbor; she was graceful, sturdy, heading for open water. She would be going to work now, to the Thalia Theatre just off Broadway at 95th Street.

"But I don't know if I want to catch up with her," he said.

"Goodbye, Carson," Leslie said. She waved to him and began to run uphill on 103rd Street, her legs pretty as a child's when she ran.

Carson started to follow her, but decided in an instant that he didn't want to do that, and turned to go uptown on Broadway, away from both women. Something bleak about the way the street looked when he headed that way touched him and chilled him again. So he turned once more, having now turned a full circle without actually moving up, down, or off the corner of Broadway and 103rd Street.

He could still see Mrs. Moore moving easily along the sidewalk, riding the flow of people. She stopped once to look in the window of a shop, and then she went on again. Carson did not think further about it. He headed after her, bumping into a crazy-looking man with shopping bags on each side of him, and then colliding with a child running uptown, but finally getting free and joining the flow of people going downtown. He would catch up with Annie before she got to the theatre, and he felt his heart be tickled with that knowledge. He straightened his tie and quickened his step.

A Dream with
No Stump Roots in It

I took a long-handled ax and made myself a stump out
of an oak tree. It felt good. My back ached for three days,
and I got a blister I kissed every morning. But I worried
about the roots of the stump that clung to the dirt beneath
my lawn. I tried not to think about them. I mowed my
grass every week and set up my croquet wickets perfectly symmetrically. But at night I dreamed about dyna-
mite, had a vision of the stump rising in the air above a
balloon of fire, the roots ripping out of the earth, and
later a beautiful flat place there where the old stump
had squatted. I dreamed my wife and I went out under
the stars and made love in the new grass that had grown
over where the roots had been. But I am a calm and inconsequential man, accustomed to living with worry.
Stump roots are nothing compared with car payments
and dentist bills. A man can live with stump roots I told
myself. I drove my car to work every morning, changed
the oil in my lawnmover after every twenty-five hours of
use, and went out each evening before dusk to pick my
ripe red tomatoes. Stump roots are nothing, I said, perhaps my child will grow up and frolic joyfully around that
old stump. Then I began to dream of strangulation, of
roots coming up through the floor of my house to choke
my wife and sweet baby while I chopped futilely at them
with my tennis racket. Don't be a fool, my wife said when
I confessed to her what troubled me. You're usually very
calm and inconsequential, she said, and I agreed. I took
my suits to the cleaners, stopped at the A&P for milk,

spaghetti sauce, and wheat germ. I took my little family on a vacation to the Jersey Shore. We stayed in a motel, splashed in the sea, became happy and sunburned. Whenever I found myself thinking that I couldn't swim because there were roots lurking just beneath the surface of the ocean, I said, don't be a fool. A week after we came home I set fire to the stump, but the flame went out in the wind. Fool, my wife said. Pyromaniac. I agreed and went to the drug store to buy aspirin for her. I built a birdhouse for the baby and tried not to look at the charred stump. We had friends over for drinks. Everybody laughed a lot when my wife told the funny story about my going out and setting fire to the stump. I did it because it was there, I said, and everybody laughed a lot. That night I woke up and walked out onto the lawn in my bare feet and pajamas. The grass was wet and cool. There was the moon, the Milky Way, the street in front of our house with a few cars driving by. There are worms and moles, too, I thought, and I took off my tops and bottoms, and laid myself flat down on the earth in the cold and wet. I wished it would rain. The paperboy came, rode his bike past me, but did not stop. The milkman came, said Hi there, and went on in his truck. At dawn my wife came out in her robe and slippers, said, What are you doing out here? Like Christ, like Lazarus, I rose, shame-faced, gathering my pajamas, looking at the imprint my body had made, a place of matted grass perfectly the shape of my body there on the lawn. I wanted to tell her, there are worms, there are moles, there are roots, but instead I said, I am ashamed, I am deeply sorry, and I slunk past her through the doorway. I was not allowed to play with the baby for three days, though I drove to work each morning, weeded the flower beds when I came home, and left generous tips for the paperboy and the milkman. Yesterday I heard my wife on the phone telling her mother the funny story about my going out in the middle of the night to lie on the lawn. Last night I dreamed my most beautiful vision: In animal skins I am walking with my wife and child over a plain of freshly mown grass. There are rows of sturdy houses and a few tennis courts in the distance. A gentle, pale blue wind is at our backs, and there is warm rich sunlight all around us. Our feet pass without sound over an earth that is smooth and endless.